THE MULTIVERSE COLLECTION

BLOODSTONE TRILOGY
BOOK ONE

LIGHT OF DEMON

BY
D. N. LEO
USA BEST SELLING AUTHOR

I0635487

Synopsis

Her mission is to serve and protect. That is, until she destroys.

When people need protection and seek help from the top mage-operating private security agent in the city, Alyna is the person for the job. On the Future Earth, where governments no longer exist, the power belongs to those who are stronger—however strength may be defined.

Caedmon is a commander with supernatural power and an army under his control. But when he travels to Future Earth on an unofficial mission, he is on his own. He could rely on Alyna for support, but what he wants might be exactly what she was built to destroy.

Bloodstone is an urban fantasy trilogy full of action with unimaginable twists and turns, magic, love, science, and war.

More information can be found at <u>http://dnleo.com</u>.

CHAPTER 1

New Earth - Distant future

Alyna tilted her head to watch the two glowing bullets flying as if in slow motion toward the two men's heads.

She had practiced her two-handed shooting skill for years but couldn't say she had ever perfected it. She would normally hit around ninety-five percent of the targets. But the remaining five percent bothered her.

She holstered her two guns and punched a button on the wall. At the far end of the shooting range, the two dummy targets glowed in a neon green light, and her shooting score hovered in the air above the targets in a light green color.

Her left-hand score was perfect, but her score from the right-hand gun wasn't so good. She had missed the head by four inches. The floating screen printed all kinds of statistics—her accuracy, her track record, her probability of hitting the target if she changed her shooting position, pose, arm movement, and even pressure on the trigger. She ignored them all.

A miss was a miss. There was nothing more to it.

She jiggled her right shoulder and felt a slight tingling in her collarbone. Perhaps Pukak was right. Amaraq, the mage tribe she had grown up with and fought for, had won battles by the sheer strength of individuals, strength magnified by martial arts skills. Pukak disliked technology and weapons of mass destruction.

But for Alyna, the ultimate aim of engaging in a fight was to win. And her simple philosophy for winning was to do whatever it took to get the win. As long as the end was morally justifiable, she needn't worry about the means. She hadn't been raised to be righteous. She had been raised to serve and protect Amaraq.

Her ear pricked at a faint noise from outside her compartment. It sounded like someone or something was shuffling through the trash cans she knew were empty.

Her compartment was one of a stack of six units right in the center of the city. It wasn't too shabby, and she'd gotten it at an affordable price. When she'd decided to buy the compartment, the deciding factor had been the extra basement where she could build her shooting room.

In two steps, she sneaked out the side door. A human-like shadow was bent over, shuffling through her neighbor's trash can.

"Hey!" she called out.

The person jerked his head up and staggered a few steps back when he saw her. Then he turned around and dashed to a nearby alleyway.

She raced after him. It wasn't much of a race because she caught up with him in no time. She grabbed him by the collar, pulling him up after he tripped and fell. He was taller than she was, but apart from that, there wasn't much in his body that would prevent her from breaking him in half with one swift move.

He struggled in her grip. "Let me go!" he cried.

"I saw you at the market," she said.

"I don't know what you're talking about."

She pushed his face into the fence with one hand and used the other to keep him still. "What's your name?"

"Don't have one."

She slammed his face against the fence.

"Ouch. Sam."

"Okay, Sam, I saw you picking pockets at the market—"

"Hey, that's none of your business."

"That's right. Otherwise, you wouldn't be standing here. I'll break your neck if you go anywhere near my people."

"Who are your people?"

"You don't need to know. But I don't want to see you near the trash cans at my compartment again."

"That's what happens when I don't pick pockets."

"How old are you?"

"It's none of your—" He looked at her raised eyebrow. "Nineteen."

"A few years late. But better late than never."

"Late for what?"

"You can join Amaraq."

Sam stepped backward. "No way." He waved his hand in the air dismissively. "I don't want that." Then he walked away.

"If you don't want it, why did you watch the open audition on the North Side? If you don't want people to know, you either don't do it, or you erase the trace properly. The door stamp is still on the nape of your neck."

"Damn it." Sam stood the neck of his jacket up to cover the mark. "I'll never make the entry comp. I'll get killed."

"What?"

"Not literally. But you know..." He flexed his skinny arm muscles, or lack thereof. "I'm not strong enough or big enough. I'll get squashed like a bug."

Alyna pulled out a couple of credit tokens she had in her pocket. "Eating food from trash cans isn't going to help you get bigger and stronger. One credit for tonight's dinner. One for tomorrow's breakfast. In the afternoon, I want to see you working at the door of the Amaraq North Side. I can give you some private training until I think you're ready for the entry comp."

"Who are you?"

"Alyna McCabe."

"You're joking. You're *the* Alyna McCabe?"

"It's the only name I have. I didn't think I was famous."

"You should hear what they say at the fighting ring."

"I'm too busy to listen to gossip. I'm not giving you these credits for free. I want them back in a week...with interest. So get working. I'll be calling Amaraq North Side in the morning. They'll be expecting you."

Sam looked at the shiny credit tokens in his palm. "Why are you helping me?"

She looked him up and down then shrugged. "Why the hell not?"

She turned, planning to head back to her shooting room, when her communicator buzzed.

"Yes, Pukak."

"Alyna, I need you at the South Side. They found a body."

She lowered her voice, looking behind her to see if Sam had followed. He hadn't. "You mean, *the* body?"

"No, another one."

"I'll be right there." She hung up the communicator and saw dust whirling up into the air in the distance. It must have come from one of the factories outside the city. The dirt must be thick since she could see it from such a distance inside the transparent dome that protected the air inside the city.

Amaraq was the strongest private security agency in the city. If they lost the city, they would have to be stationed on the outskirts, out there in in that whirling lump of dirt.

CHAPTER 2

Polluted. That was the first impression Caedmon had when he stepped out of the portal to New Earth. They called it New Earth, but it wasn't so much different than when he had been with Sedna in Greenland. He should have treasured every moment he'd had with her. He shook his head to escape his brooding mood. He couldn't afford that right now.

Focus. He had come to the future only to alter his past reality. One wrong move and he'd be stuck in this future oblivion forever.

He could still feel the sensation of the heatwave from the explosion—the one that had robbed him of his family, and the multiverse of the precious traces to the Scorpio key.

He had reminded himself every waking moment over the last month about the mission he had to fulfill by coming here. He was a commander with Silver Blood energy—a special source of energy that could destroy almost anything in its way. An important skill he had learned over the years was to control the energy so he could use its destructive power against those who deserved it. But he knew his disadvantage when coming to Earth from Eudaiz, a faraway universe, and being on his own.

His father had approved of his mission but wouldn't have approved of the way he had approached it. Thus, he had no military support. The injury his father had suffered from the explosion had limited his capacity to work for a few weeks, Eudaizian time. That means he'd have years on Earth to execute his plan.

He stepped into a corporate transport, a hovering private car that was waiting for him. Inside, he was greeted by a computer screen that flashed a scanner beam at him and then faded away immediately once it recognized him.

Apparently, asking for consent wasn't a part of the identification process on New Earth. There was definitely room for system improvement, but he had no attachment to Earth, neither the old one nor the new one. And he had his own problem to deal with.

He punched the green start button on the control panel. As the car automatically departed the station and drove itself, he settled next to the window to look outside. He saw nothing but red dirt. The multiversal teleport terminal must be quite a distance from where people lived.

After a while, the transport crossed a transparent dome that covered what looked like a city. It was similar to London, New York, and other places he had been to when he'd visited Earth before. But he didn't recognize any of the landmarks here, and the liquid map on the dashboard didn't show the shape or size of any of the countries.

He could have done a more thorough investigation of the place before he came, but he had been using a rather shady source of information to get what he needed, so he was in and out of the databank too quickly to obtain anything more than the bare essentials.

There it was, the LeBlanc headquarters in the center of the city, in a small but exclusive area called Old Sydney. It was apparently a piece of what used to be Sydney, a city in Australia if his memory served him right. Some of the landmark's architecture had been preserved and treated like rare pieces of art in a museum. It was quite charming.

The floor-to-ceiling steel door slid open as he approached. He noted that the lightweight steel his father had invented when he was a kid had been used for the office door. It looked just like any other door, but the properties of this steel could protect the people inside from a multiversal war of the worst kind.

A stunning woman approached him. "Mr. LeBlanc, welcome!"

"Caedmon, please," he said and glanced at his wrist unit, which by that point had scanned and identified the woman as his executive secretary. "It's very nice to meet you, Leanne."

"It's an honor to be at your service, Mr.—" She hesitated then smiled graciously. "Caedmon. The LeBlancs have never before sent a representative to this corner of the Earth."

"I'm happy to be here. We need to interact much more with our associated branches."

She gestured to a smaller steel door, and he guessed his office was inside. "I have arranged everything you need inside," she said. "Your computer, your workstation. Also, food and beverages are there as well."

"Food and beverage?"

"Oh, I don't know about Mid-Land London, but eating the wrong foods here can have nasty consequences, especially for out-of-towners. If you need more, I've programmed your contacts. Just call for service, and whatever you need will be delivered to you. Please don't wander around the city, especially in the unsavory areas, without a security escort."

"I can take care of myself."

"I'm more than sure you can, Caedmon. But it's my top priority to make sure you are safe."

"You seem so tense. You're making me feel unsafe already."

"Really? I'm so sorry. I didn't mean to—"

"Leanne, I'm just joking. Relax."

"I'll try." She smiled.

"Okay, just to make you feel better, I promise not to head into any bad parts of the city, okay? So what places are at the top of that list?"

"The North Side."

"All right, North Side it is." He grinned at her and was pleased to see her relax a bit more. But then her shoulders tensed up, and her smile vanished. "Mr. Tann," she whimpered and looked down.

Caedmon turned around. An intimidating man with a hard face and a scar along his left jawline approached, reaching his hand out for a handshake.

"I'm Lewis Tann."

Caedmon smiled. "The man in charge!"

Lewis smiled. "Only when you're not here. To what do we owe a visit from the Mid-Land London central, Mr. LeBlanc?"

"Don't worry, I won't be in your way for long. I guess that's where my temporary office is?" He pointed at the steel door.

"Sure is. As permanent or temporary as you'd like it." Lewis gestured for Caedmon to go ahead of him.

Caedmon turned and grinned at Leanne. "I promise I'll only eat the food you recommend."

Leanne smiled then looked down when her eyes fell on Lewis.

On the way into the office, Caedmon quickly scanned the area for the layout, entry and exit points, and number of staff.

"I trust you received the memos, Mr. Tann?"

"Yes, and I still don't understand them. The business here is doing well. Why do we need to take on Amaraq's burdens?"

"It's called a business extension."

"Look, Caedmon, private security business isn't our thing. We're not into fist fights and gang business."

"But it can be lucrative if done the right way. That is, using advanced technology and weapons street gangs can't afford. And it's the LeBlanc's profits we're talking about here."

"Yes, but it's not a safe business."

"Are you suggesting we should start selling flowers?

"LeBlanc Pharmaceuticals is our strongest business line. Why deviate from that?"

Caedmon smiled. "You obviously haven't gotten the full picture of the takeover proposal, Mr. Tann. Amaraq has two main businesses, and the private security business is a by-product for me. I am interested in their natural medicine business, which is bankrupting them at the moment."

"How do you know that?"

"Because I'm from Mid-Land London. You don't have anything to worry about, Mr. Tann. If I turn

Amaraq's natural medicine business into a success, you'll keep your job doing whatever you do here."

Mr. Tann nodded.

"I'll need to survey the area along with the clinics, so I'm going to take a walk around. Where do you suggest I look first, Mr. Tann?"

Lewis Tann smiled. "The North Side."

"The North Side it is. I'll let you know what I find."

Mr. Tann nodded a goodbye and strode out of the office.

CHAPTER 3

Alyna walked into a small natural medicine clinic that Pukak managed and used as his office on the North Side of the city. She knocked on the crooked office door, but there was no answer, so she pushed her way in.

Pukak was the leader of the clan, a powerful mage with ultra-sensitive ears that could hear faint sounds even a mile away, and his light energy could burn the entire block of compartments.

Well, that had been during his heyday. He was nearly retired now. Or if Alyna understood him right, he could retire if he found a rightful successor for the clan.

But he cared too much to let go.

Pukak startled and jerked up from his chair. "Don't you know how to knock, Alyna?"

"I did, but you seemed to be too busy sniffing your piles of paper to hear me."

He rubbed at his temples and leaned back in his chair. She noted the bags under his eyes. He looked ten years older than when she had seen him yesterday.

"Is everything okay...apart from the two dead bodies?"

He shook his head and sighed.

"I have friends in the investigation business uptown," she said. "They can help."

"What's the point, Alyna? Ethesus wants to ruin us. If they don't do it in one way, they'll find another."

"Pukak, we are the best in the business. There is nothing a bunch of scumbags on wheels like Ethesus could do to threaten us."

"We are the best in the private security business, but not in natural medicine. Ethesus is the second best at everything in the outskirt territories."

"I thought medicine was just a small business..."

Pukak shook his head. His eyes drooped, and with that, the skin on his face sagged even more. "It's small because I failed. With today's technology, people don't appreciate natural medicine anymore."

She approached the table. She wanted to do something to comfort him, but she always felt awkward when it came to showing compassion. She could help with a fight. She could physically protect him. But she didn't know how to help when it came to his sentimental attachment to Amaraq.

"Have you given the successor role some more thought?" he asked.

"No, I'm sorry." She shoved her hands in her pockets. "I'm not a mage."

Pukak chuckled. "As if I didn't know that! Thank you for the reminder. I've been taking care of you since you were sixteen. You're my protege. Nobody says the successor has to be a mage. We elect by competition. And you are the best, Alyna."

"I'm only good at combat, Pukak. As you said, the business is more complicated than that. I don't think I'm fit for the role."

He nodded. "If that's the only reason."

"What do you mean?"

"You're not an ordinary human. You know that, Alyna."

"I don't know that."

"No human could have survived that car crash. Your parents died. When I pulled you out of the wreck, I swear to you I saw your light go out for a moment and then return."

"You told me that, and I don't have an explanation for you. Maybe it was a near death experience. But it still doesn't make me anything different from how I was created."

"You're absolutely right. But I am an old mage. I have seen a lot of things you couldn't imagine. And I can see the dark energy in you. Something returned with you during that experience."

"Yes, Pukak, you've said that several times. But I don't have any supernatural power. That much I know. The blow I took from the Ethesus thug the other week injured my right shoulder. I didn't get away unscathed. And if I'm ever in another car crash, I'm pretty sure you won't pull me out alive."

"All right, all right, I won't push you. Anything new about the dead body?"

She shook her head. "If the death toll rises, it will set the private security business on fire, Pukak. And it's not just the business...we can't let them kill our people. We have to stop Ethesus. We have the manpower."

"We can't go to war with them for no reason. We have no evidence they have killed our men."

"I can—"

"No, Alyna. We can't afford to lose you. I don't approve of you going anywhere near Ethesus territories by yourself. If we fight them, we must be better prepared. They have the wheels, but we will have weapons."

"It's about damn time."

"Excuse me?"

"I mean, it's only fair if we get more guns. Fist fighting against a motorbike gang won't do us any good."

Pukak nodded. "I understand. We're skilled fighters, but yes, weapons help. But they cost money." He looked at her with eyes that told her she was about to hear something she didn't want to. "I've sold Amaraq's business."

She didn't know what to say, so she remained silent.

"Our spiritual practice will stay the same. We'll still operate the same way. It's just that the financial matters and business practices will be handled by the LeBlanc Group."

"The LeBlancs? The super uptown, living-in-the-cloud-with-the-gods LeBlancs?"

Pukak chuckled. "They're not that elusive. In fact, one of the LeBlancs handled the business purchase himself—he didn't even send his minions. He's coming here to do a site visitation."

"You're kidding!"

"No, I'm not. The contract is still in the cooling-off period, so we'd better behave, Alyna. We need the money for the business. And I promise you, Amaraq's spirit will stay the same. Nothing's going to change that. The LeBlancs aren't interested in our spiritual practice anyway. They vetted us carefully. I've done my homework, too."

"I'm sure you know what you're doing."

"I can't do it without you. Now I need you to host the visit for me."

"Host? Me? What do you mean?"

"Well, we have dirty laundry to hide, don't we? I'm not asking you to lie. All I'm asking is that you get them to see the negative aspects of the business in perspective."

"Got it."

They heard a knock on the door.

"And here he is," Pukak muttered and stood up. "The door is open."

Alyna turned around, and in front of her was a face that left her speechless.

She had seen him before.

For a week, she had seen his face repeatedly in her dreams, dreams that woke her up in the middle of the night. Longish dark hair, strikingly haunting gray eyes, and a beautiful God-given face that didn't bear any mark of a hard life.

He straightened his posture after bending over to get through the low doorway. "Hello," he said.

She swiveled to his right side, reached her hand up, and stopped his head an inch before it hit the broken low-hanging ceiling lamp.

As she moved, the photos of the dead bodies she had just taken slid out of the folder in her hand and landed on the dirty floor in front of him.

He glanced at the photos and looked at her, smiling, "Thank you. Caedmon LeBlanc." He reached his hand out to shake hers.

She shook his hand quickly and bent down to pick up the photos. Pukak wanted to walk around the table for a handshake, but there was no room, so he reached over and across it.

Caedmon advanced to the table to shake his hand. Pukak's elbow hit the pile of papers on his table, scattering them all over the floor. Photos, unpaid bills, an eviction notice from the building owner, complaint letters about water leakage from citizens living around a clinic in midtown drifted all over the room.

Alayna scrambled on all fours to pick up as many pieces of paper as possible.

Caedmon crouched. "Let me help," he said.

Pukak pushed his way to the front. "Oh no, no, it's okay. I'll handle this. Alyna," he said. "Please take Mr. LeBlanc to visit the clinic in midtown. The one that's open today."

That means the one that doesn't have water leakage, she thought and winked at Pukak.

Caedmon stood up.

"Go, both of you. You're crowding my office." Pukak was all but pushing Caedmon and Alayna out of his office.

"All right," Caedmon said and turned to the door. Then he sneezed because of the dust, lost his balance, and hit his head on the low doorway on his way out.

"Are you okay?" Alayna asked.

He rubbed his head and grinned.

What a smile! she thought.

"My father always told me I have a hard head."

"You might, but still...competing with a doorframe isn't a good idea."

"Totally agree."

Before she could react, he slid his arm around her waist and guided her out. She felt like a true lady.

"Now, is someone killing your men? Those dead men in the photos were Amaraq fighters, right?"

CHAPTER 4

The beginning of time.

He picked up a shard of ice that shone a deep blood red. It wasn't just ice. It was frozen dragon blood.

He glanced behind him and saw that Thunder Child was still sleeping soundly next to a large rock. It had taken them days to get here, and she was tired. He should give her a better name than

Thunder Child, but he had no idea what to call her. He didn't even have a name for himself.

People called him Keymaster because he made keys. Not just any keys. His keys unlocked the sources of energy and power, unlocked the doors between worlds. He considered himself an artist in the key-making business, and thus, he didn't come cheap. If creatures in the multiverse needed his keys and couldn't afford them, they'd kill to get them. And to that extent, he knew he had indirectly created some chaos and casualties in the multiverse.

But it was just business. He got paid to make keys. That was all he did. He couldn't control what people did with the products they had paid for.

He couldn't even remember how many keys he had created. A few hundred maybe. Some were more difficult to make than others. But this one might be the most difficult one—the Scorpio key.

He chipped into the large piece of ice to break it into several shards that he could transport easily. The freezing conditions weren't ideal. He needed to get the ice back to his studio so that he could work.

He went back to the child and tucked the cloak around her to keep her warm. He brushed aside the hair on her forehead. She was beautiful. She was a child born of angels, after all, and he wouldn't expect less when it came to her beauty. She must be eight now, or maybe seven. He'd lost track of time.

He had picked her up as an infant, sitting next to the dead body of her mother, clapping her little hands and flapping her tiny wings. Before he knew it, she had given him instructions on how to make some of the more difficult keys and had become a significant part of his life. And just now, she had showed him the way to the rock of dragon blood.

He kept telling her she could go to the Daimon Gate or go back to the angels. But she preferred to stay with him.

She winced in her sleep, and he knew what was coming. He picked her up in his arms and clutched her tight. "Come on, don't do that to yourself, child."

Her shoulders twisted, and her body shook. Tears rolled down her face. He held her tighter. Otherwise, she would clap her hands together, and the thunder would come. He had seen that before. Her thunder could devastate a mountain.

Her nightmares came often, and it pained him as much as it tormented her. She never talked about it. But he knew she had seen what killed her parents, and it haunted her dreams. The older she grew, the more frequently the nightmares came. But if she wouldn't talk about it, there was nothing he could do for her.

Her body shook for a while then eased off. He lay her down and wiped the sweat from her beautiful young face.

"One day you will tell me what killed your parents, Thunder Child," he said.

Her eyes fluttered and then opened. She smiled at him. "Did you find the blood rock?"

"Yes, right over there."

She sat up and looked in the direction he pointed. A smile brightened her angelic face. She rushed toward the rock and traced her little fingers along the rough edges of the ice shards.

She remembered nothing about the dream she'd just had or how much she had shaken in his arms. She had no conscious recollection of her parents' violent death. Yet in dreams, it came back to haunt her. Perhaps she remembered but didn't let on. There had been so many times he'd wanted to ask her. But he had no clue when she would be old enough to handle such a conversation, so he always let the thought go.

She turned around and smiled at him. "Bloodstone." She grinned again and raised her hands.

"No, no, don't clap. You know you have a clapping disorder, don't you?"

She giggled and then put her hands down.

He exhaled in relief and flopped down, leaning against the rock she had just slept next to. That was his eternal nightmare. He didn't know when one of her thunder strikes would explode him right out of his immortal life.

She shrugged then picked up his hunting knife and used it to chip away at the rock. A thin stream of red liquid leaked out.

"Look, Keymaster." She pointed.

He approached. "Holy cow. The rock is bleeding. It's dragon's blood," he said.

"No, Keymaster, not dragon's blood. It's scorpion."

"Scorpions don't have blood."

"It's King Scorpion's blood. He used to be a man."

He staggered back. "Are you sure? Is he in there?"

"No, it was just his heart and his head."

"How do you know that?"

"It comes to me in my dreams, Keymaster."

"Oh, those dreams. All right. As long as a giant scorpion isn't going to crawl out of that stone to bite me, I'm fine. I hate insects. I only need the rocks to make the key. I have no need for a bleeding heart. Let me chip away some more rocks, and then we'll leave for home."

"For the Scorpio key, you'll need some blood from the heart, too."

"How do you—" He stopped himself. "All right, knowledge from the dreams, right? But how long will it take me to chip away that giant rock to the heart of the Scorpion?"

"I'll do it for you. One strike." She smiled graciously.

"You'll just use any excuse to clap that thunder out of your little hands. Okay, don't pout. I'll let you do it. But let me find shelter first." He scurried away to a nearby cave and crawled inside as deep as he could. "All right, I'm safe," he called.

He heard her giggle, and then an explosion of thunder that almost punctured his eardrums echoed through the air. Everything went quiet.

He stepped outside and saw a massive hole in the ground. Thunder Child stood next to a neatly cut giant piece of bloodstone. She smiled at him.

"Where are the heart and the head?" he asked.

She pointed at the piece of icy red rock. "In there. It's all done for you, Keymaster."

CHAPTER 5

"Sushi?" Alyna asked.

"Excuse me?" Caedmon turned toward her. He had been looking at the billboard hanging from a tall building, advertising exotic holiday deals to Nepolymbus. It fascinated him. Not the holiday deals, but the development of New Earth since the years he had known it. Nepolymbus had been a submarine dimension that was at war with humans. But if they were now organizing tours there, they must have made peace at some point.

"I asked if you're hungry."

"No, thank you. But I can wait if you need to eat." He chuckled on the inside, remembering how his secretary, Leanne, had warned him about food consumption.

She smiled at him. "I only need five minutes." She tapped a small device on her belt. "I have to maintain a regular intake of necessary nutrition. There's no magic when it comes to strength and fitness." Then she walked across the road to what looked like a street food vendor.

She must be a hell of a fighter, he thought. Her long and agile body glided across the street with ease. Her long hair was pulled back tightly into a braided ponytail that swung between her shoulders. He thought her hair to be flattering and flirty at times, but he was sure she didn't think about it that way. Her dress code and posture was combat-ready. He had seen it in some of his female commanders, and he knew enough to not mess around with them.

The street looked just like Midtown New York. He had never been, but he had done a quick scan of the data and possible locations before embarking on this trip. Unfortunately, his data seemed to be quite outdated.

In about three minutes, Alyna came back to him. "Done already?"

"It wasn't exactly a three-course lunch."

"Are there places that have such offers?"

She laughed. "So you're hungry, but you're not quite into street food."

"I was told to be careful about what I eat."

"And you are absolutely right to do so. This is midtown, so it's not too bad. But I'll take you to a place uptown, and then you can have whatever you need." She gestured ahead. "The clinic is just around the corner."

"Thank you."

As they walked toward the clinic, he discreetly turned on his eudqi—a special source of Eudaizian energy designed just for him. With that activated, he had access to a personal micro internal computer system that could perform various small tasks. He snapped a scan of the area and recorded the map. Then he turned the system off and switched back to his normal operational mode.

In normal mode, he had a human body with Eudaizian energy.

He saw the clinic at the end of the small side road. It looked quite charming from the outside.

Alyna's communicator buzzed, and she picked it up. Then her face paled.

"What is it, Alyna?"

"Just a problem with the security business. Given that's not what you're interested in, let's just take a look at the clinic, and then I'll take you back to where you're staying."

"The call you just received, is it urgent?" He locked eyes with her to let her know he wouldn't like it if she withheld information from him.

She nodded. "It's urgent. But your interest lies in the natural medicine clinics, so—"

"I'm paying for the whole lot, Alyna. That includes the private security business as well. Not only do I need an answer now about what's just happened, but I also need answers from you about the dead men in the photos this morning."

"Pukak said you were going to leave our operation alone and only assist with financial matters."

"No, what I said was I'll leave your spiritual practice and beliefs alone. I know Amaraq is a mage-operating organization. I respect that. But I'll handle any operational matter that has financial implications. And I'm guessing having your men die in the line of duty has an implication for the private security business. Am I correct?"

She looked at him, hesitating. "Have you seen a dead body before?"

He'd been to battles before. He had no idea how many thousands of space creatures he had killed. Caedmon's face remained stoic as he said, "No, but I'm educated, I have medical knowledge, and I can handle seeing dead bodies. So...what was the call about?"

Alyna waved her arms in the air in frustration. "Pukak won't like this!"

"If you want my money in the business, I need to know everything about it. Otherwise, I'm out."

She sighed. "It's a client. His son has just been found dead."

"We provide a private security service, and a client's son is dead, and you didn't think it was in my interest to know?"

"Well, you know now!"

"Have you called the authorities?"

"I just found out about it now. I haven't called Pukak, but you're the authority now." She paced back and forth in agitation.

"Give me a minute." He turned away, pretending to think, and discreetly switched on his microcomputer again. He searched for general information about New Earth in his current location at the current time. The command was simple, and he didn't think there was any danger of overloading the microchip. Instantly, a stream of information appeared in his mind's eye.

He scanned the information. Then he switched it off and turned back to look at Alyna. He didn't know what to say.

This was New Earth, 2999. There was no government or authority of any kind here. Commerce operated on total freedom of supply and demand. People hired private security for protection. The people were the authority over themselves.

He didn't know he had traveled so far into the Future Earth. But that was beside the point. The system had calculated that the Scorpio key was here. At this time, and in this location now called New Earth.

"Caedmon?"

"Yes."

"What's your decision? If you take the business, then you're the one in charge."

"Right. We'll have to see the dead body first and talk to the client. The father must be devastated."

Alyna shook her head.

"You mean he doesn't care?" he asked.

She looked at him, and he could see an ocean of sadness in those deep emerald eyes. She bit her lips lightly. He figured that was to prevent unwanted tears.

"Tony is seventeen, and he could have done a lot better if not for the scumbag he calls a brother. His father is on his deathbed, and his wealth has been distributed evenly between his two sons. Tony's money is with a financial guardian until he's eighteen. His father—when he was still conscious—hired us to protect Tony. See what he's gotten his son?"

A tear rolled down her face, and she wiped it off quickly.

Caedmon tried to touch her shoulder in comfort, but she shrugged him off.

"So to answer your question, no, his father won't feel any pain. He's in a coma now, waiting to die. As for the money, we'll lose it because his brother will take the business to Ethesus."

"I don't care about the money."

"I don't, either. And not because it's not my money. But this is just the beginning. I told Pukak, Ethesus will do whatever it takes to destroy us."

"I take it they're our competitor."

"Yes. And if they take over the city, it will be chaos. More than we've already seen."

"How so?"

"They worship Satan."

CHAPTER 6

Alyna didn't need to verify the security code at the door to enter Tony's residence. The young man was dead, and the door was wide open. Amaraq had already sent people to investigate the cause of death and the potential killer. If they had found evidence, they had the authority to execute the killer.

Ben, notepad in hand, approached from a side corridor. Ben was in his mid-thirties and had been with Amaraq since he was a teenager. Like many other young teens, he had joined to learn martial arts and survival techniques to protect himself. Then he began to conduct the business to protect others. Alyna trusted him.

"He's in the lunch room. There's no trace of a wound, Alyna." Ben glanced at Caedmon and stopped talking.

"This is Caedmon LeBlanc. He's our new business owner."

"What do you mean? You and Pukak won't be with us any longer?"

Caedmon reached his hand out for a handshake, but Ben raised his hand, showing him the thin coat of transparent substance covering it. "I'm wearing a protective shield to examine the dead body," he explained.

Caedmon nodded and said, "Alyna and Pukak aren't going anywhere. I'm just assisting with some financial matters." He gestured widely around the room. "And learning the business, of course."

When Ben looked at Alyna, she gave him a nod of approval, so he continued. "Tony was probably killed just an hour ago," he said, "and I'm guessing it was because of the suppression of air to his brain."

"He was strangled?" Alyna asked.

"There were no marks. No sign of a physical struggle. And there was no poison in his system that I can detect so far. But his heart failed, and his brain reacted as if there was a lack of oxygen. I'm not sure of the sequence—whether his heart or his brain failed first—but it's all speculation because there were no physical marks on his body whatsoever. It was as if…" He trailed off.

Alyna raised an eyebrow, waiting. Ben looked from Alyna to Caedmon.

"This is just my opinion," he said. "I don't have any evidence to back this up."

"Spit it out, Ben," Alyna said.

"It was as if the life was sucked out of him."

"What do you mean?" Caedmon asked. "If he didn't die naturally, then someone took his life. That's obvious."

Ben rocked back and forth from his heels to the balls of his feet. "It's like his soul, or his spirit, was taken from him."

Alyna shook her head as she strode into the adjacent room via a side hallway. The room was spacious and filled with natural sunlight via a large floor-to-ceiling glass window. She saw the table where Tony had loved to sit to have his meals, watch the screen, and read old comic books he got from an antique collection in the museum. He had been planning to reprint those books with real paper—regardless of how expensive it would be to do so. The books were still there, scattered all over the floor. He must have pushed them to the floor as he fell.

Tony's body was on the floor. He looked as if he were sleeping peacefully. He had been so young and full of life.

She approached and crouched next to the body. On his knuckles were the bruises she had put there. He had started taking martial art lessons with her because he didn't like being surrounded by security all the time.

Then, from the body in front of her, a whirl of black smoke and semitransparent particles surged up from the ground to form the wriggling shape of a man, his hands reaching out to grab her neck.

She staggered back, falling to the floor. She gasped. She couldn't breathe. She tried to yank the hands off her neck, but they weren't tangible, and there was nothing for her to grab. But her windpipe was closing. That much she knew.

Her vision blurred quickly as her air was cut off. She saw Caedmon and Ben panicking, saying something she could neither hear nor understand. Her world was dimming by the second. She felt Caedmon's hands on her shoulders. He said something.

Then her world went completely dark.

She felt a zap, like a spark of electric current tearing through her body. Then came another one. And another.

Blood and air started to circulate once again. She felt her body operating on its own. She opened her eyes and saw Caedmon's face over hers. She guessed he had done something to save her. She wanted to say thank you, or at least smile, but her body didn't want to cooperate.

"All right, I'll take her back to her place," Caedmon said then lifted her up into his arms. She was five foot eleven, yet he lifted her up like she was as light as a little girl's doll. She couldn't move at the moment, so she let her head loll on his strong shoulder.

When Caedmon turned around, she saw the concern look on Ben's face. She understood. She felt as though she had just come back from death. She was tired, so she closed her eyes.

"It's in your best interest to forget what you saw me do, Ben," Caedmon said.

"I'll have to tell Pukak."

"You don't have to do anything. If you say a word, I'll withdraw my business offer to Amaraq. Talk to Pukak instead about the consequence of not having my financial backing. Understood?"

"Yes."

Alyna felt movement. Then she heard the sound of traffic. She stirred and opened her eyes.

"There you are. Ben said I should take you home and not to a medical center. But I have no idea where you live. Let me have look at your ID card."

A cab stopped right next to them. He climbed in with ease and settled Alyna on his lap.

"Sorry," he said as he stuck his hand into her pants pocket and pulled out her ID. He gave the address to the driver.

She was so glad she lived in the center of the town and not in a dump somewhere on the outskirts. The downside of the location, however, was that her rent chewed up a large part of her wages. As the car moved, her face pressed into Caedmon's chest. She could smell his masculinity. She had been with men before, but this was the most sensual scent she had ever experienced. She was embarrassed, yet unable to move her head away from his chest.

A short moment later, he carried her into the bedroom in her apartment and put her gently on her bed.

"I can see you're now able to blink those pretty eyes of yours. But they need to rest." He took her boots off and sat down at her bedside. "I'll loosen this braided ponytail. It's too tight."

He tugged at it and loosened her hair a bit.

"Don't panic, I'm not going to undress you. But this belt's got to go." He took her belt off. "Also, I have to loosen this as well. You can beat me up for this when you can move again." He slid his arms around her back and unclasped her bra.

He then wrapped the blanket around her, dimmed the light, and left the room.

She lay there, staring at the ceiling and digesting what had just happened. She rested, waiting for her muscles to strengthen, cell by cell. She could still smell his scent hovering in the air of her bedroom.

Damn it. She closed her eyes for a bit. Then she concentrated on her muscle movements again.

CHAPTER 7

Caedmon wasn't keen on square buildings. But he wasn't going to find the grand rooms and high-ceilinged towers of Eudaiz anywhere else in the multiverse. He glanced back at the bedroom door and was sure Alyna was still resting. He needed his privacy, but he couldn't leave her alone in her current condition.

His stomach growled. He was really hungry. But he had work to do, and he had to make use of the little space he had available in this compartment.

He settled at the kitchen table and turned on his wrist unit. He entered a command, and the face of Lorcan Brody, a wicked technology head in the Daimon Gate appeared.

Lorcan frowned. "Ciaran?"

"I guess I look like my father."

"Holy cow, you're Caedmon. The unit just said LeBlanc, so I assumed... Wait, so you're calling from the future? What're you doing?"

"Uncle Lorcan, I need your and Orla's help."

"That much I can guess. But you're not contacting us in the future, so does that mean we're dead?"

"No, no, I need you at your current time. Would you mind getting Aunty Orla so I can explain this only once? I haven't got much time."

Orla's exotic voice sounded, and her beautiful face loomed on the screen. "I heard my name. Hello there, Caedmon. You've grown into a fine man. Calling from the future, are you?"

Lorcan gasped. "How could you tell it was him. Why didn't you think it was Ciaran?"

Orla shrugged. "Well, they do look alike. But Ciaran doesn't have that twinkle in the eyes. You can never tell what Ciaran's thinking. Charming Caedmon here can never hide his emotions."

Lorcan rolled his eyes. "Women."

He must have earned a pinch from Orla for that comment because he yelped.

"What do you need, Caedmon?" Orla asked.

"I need Uncle Lorcan to find out, at your current time now, whether my father has obtained the Scorpio key. If not, that's the right time point."

Lorcan turned to another monitor, returning shortly. "No. Ciaran and Madeline have just obtained the Virgo key. There's a note, confidential of course, about another five keys. Scorpio is one of them."

Caedmon nodded. "All right. In the future, I figured out that my father failed to obtain the Scorpio key, and the consequence was disastrous. I traveled to the past, just before he went for the key, and offered to go in his place. I got the key, married Sedna, and came back to my future. Am I confusing you yet?"

Orla shook her head. "Something happened to your wife, didn't it?" Tears gleamed in her eyes.

"Caedmon, stop crying. Tears are contagious," Lorcan said.

Caedmon didn't realize tears had rolled down his face, and he had made Orla emotional. He wiped them away. "Sorry. I can't control this." Then he looked at Orla. "Yes, Aunty Orla, something happened to my wife. A month ago—in the future that is. I don't know how, but she figured out that the Scorpio key we obtained was fake. She traveled back to the past to the point when she

55

had just given the key to my father, and she asked for it back. Could you excuse me for just a sec…"

He went into the bathroom and splashed cold water onto his face. He couldn't control his emotional and chemical reactions, but that didn't mean he was mentally weak. Sedna always teased him when he encountered emotional news, and his chemical reaction triggered tears he couldn't control. He would improve over time. But she hadn't had a chance to see that, had she? He inhaled deeply to gather himself together and then stepped back out to the kitchen.

He looked into the screen again so that Lorcan and Orla could see his face and know he had composed himself. He spoke with clarity. "I didn't know Sedna's plan when she took the fake key back. She jumped into an ice oblivion hole, and then there was an explosion from the hole."

"And you can't accept that she might be dead. That's why you are where you are now?" Lorcan asked.

Caedmon nodded. "Until I find evidence, I won't believe she's dead. Because I've traveled to the past and cheated fate to get the key, I can't travel back to fix the future consequences of my own action. So instead, I traveled further into the future, to here and now."

"Interesting plan, Caedmon. What's your theory?" Lorcan asked.

"Sedna is a mage. Her mage tribe worships the Scorpio key. When we took the key and left, the tribe was supposed to dissolve. But they didn't. They transformed and now are operating under the name Amaraq. And they still worship the Scorpio key."

"The real key?" Orla asked.

"I don't know. My plan is to get into the mage tribe, find the person who swapped the real key, and make him or her—or *it*—go back to the past and place the real key in the temple at a time before we got the key. I can't travel to the past, but I can send that person—or thing—back."

"It's good in theory, but how do you plan to make the thing agree to travel?"

"All things want to stay alive. It can stay here and die with the key, or travel back to the past to replace the key and live. I will hold whatever is important to it here at ransom."

"You'd kill for this, Caedmon?" Orla asked.

"It's not just my wife's life. If the key falls into the wrong hands, many people will die. My father said the set of six keys connects multiple worlds and gives the connector the ultimate power. And Hoyt Flanagan is working to get all six of the keys. I have to get to the key before he does."

"Flanagan?" Orla shook her head and shuddered. "You'd better get that key, Caedmon."

"So if you already have a plan, how can we help?" Lorcan asked.

"I've done my research, roughly, and understand how a mage's magic works. But just now, I saw a form of dematerialization."

"That's your Uncle Tadgh's talent," Lorcan said.

"Yes, and Hoyt Flanagan's. But Hoyt is a lot more seasoned than my uncle."

"Yes, he's got a few hundred years on Tadgh. Plus he practices dark magic. Is that why you want me?" Orla asked.

Caedmon nodded. "Yes, your experience with sorcery is much needed. But I dare not ask you to perform a ritual inside the Daimon Gate. All I need now is a spell or something I can use to protect myself if dark magic is used against me."

Orla smiled. "You're a thousand times more open-minded than your father, Caedmon. Yes, I can work on that for you."

"And Uncle Lorcan, could you please find out what the group called Ethesus does? Do they have anything to do with Satan? And is Satan a branch of religious belief or a kind of magic? At your current time now, could you triangulate to equivalent Earth time and figure out if there's a surge of multiversal energy in Greenland and the Arctic? I focused only on the mage tribe and neglected everything beyond that."

Lorcan raised an eyebrow. "I assume you don't want the info from the ordinary databank because you could just do that search yourself. You want me to use our *special source*, right?"

By special source, Caedmon meant the wicked databank of the multiverse called the EYE. Even his father didn't have access to it. Getting caught stealing data from the EYE was a grave offense.

Caedmon nodded.

"Like father, like son," Lorcan muttered. "Your father had the same look on his face when he wanted me to do the same thing."

"Please?"

"All right. It'll take some time. I'll get back to you, and— Holy cow! You're in 2999 Earth time. Look, Orla!" Lorcan pointed at the screen.

Orla narrowed her eyes. "Do you know what it means to practice magic, Caedmon?"

"No. All I know is that the computer simulation told me the real Scorpio key is here, in this time and close to this place." He rolled his eyes. "By this place, I mean New Earth."

Orla nodded. "Now I've got more to do."

Caedmon heard footsteps. "I've got to go. Oh, just so you know, here I'm just a human, a filthy rich LeBlanc buying Amaraq's business. So if you need to contact me, please don't flash the holocast when I'm in public."

As soon as he turned his communicator off, Pukak kicked the door in.

Before Caedmon could do anything, a light beam struck him, and he was thrown into the opposite wall.

CHAPTER 8

Keymaster would be asleep for a little longer. He always took long naps in the afternoon. And the making of the Scorpio key seemed to be more taxing for him than the other keys he'd made. The bloodstone must be harder to carve.

She checked for one last time to ensure he was sleeping soundly, then she sneaked through the back door of the small hut and ran into the nearby forest.

It had been eight long years, and she still remembered the sound of the flesh being torn from her mother's body as she was slaughtered. They didn't think an infant could possibly have had awareness or any memory about the incident. Because of that, they hadn't killed her. They had shown mercy.

She wished otherwise.

It was too far for her to travel back to the stone mountain where her parents were murdered. So every day, for as long as she had been able, she came here to this small cave, to remember and to plan her revenge.

Revenge our death, our sweet child. Remember, we love you. Forever. She repeated her mother's last words every time she was in this cave.

She didn't know her name, but she was happy with what Keymaster called her. Thunder Child. It sounded strong. She smiled to herself. Keymaster had always thought of himself as a predator, but he didn't realize how sweet he was with children. She had never seen him kill any creature that hadn't deserved to die.

On that note, he wouldn't be happy to see what she was doing in this cave. She took out a knife she kept hidden underneath a stone. It was the hunting knife he thought he had lost. She clambered out of the cave and went hunting. The creatures in the woods that she would kill today to practice her fighting skills were innocent. But she had to practice. She had to hone her skills. When she faced the murderers of her parents, she would be on her own. She would kill them will her own hands.

She raced through the woods. There—she saw a movement. She chased the shadow. It was a four-legged creature. Furry. Black and gray. She didn't know what it was, but it ran, and she chased. In no time, she had caught up with it. Her skills were improving. She ran faster every day. And she became stronger every day.

She got close enough to recognize that it was a wolf she was chasing. Wolves were dangerous animals. She could kill it.

She jumped in the air, stabbed downward, and caught the animal in its tracks. It was on the ground, kicking its legs in pain, uttering desperate noises. She stepped up to it to finish the job, but then she heard faint whining noises and saw three small pups by a nearby tree. The mother wolf turned and looked at her with big brown eyes and let out a mournful sound.

She always finished the job. But maybe not today.

She let the wolf get up. As soon as it regained its footing, it raced to the pups, and together, they ran away.

"That was weak," an elderly male voice said from behind her.

She yelped, jumped aside, and swung the knife upward. A tall man with red eyes and long white hair in a long black cloak grabbed her wrist and twisted the knife out of her hand.

"Who are you?"

"I am your teacher."

"Keymaster is my teacher."

"He doesn't teach you how to seek revenge. He doesn't teach you how to kill or how to survive."

"Why do you want to teach me?"

"Let's say we share some common enemies. I am bound by a curse and can't kill those I need to. But you can do it for me. So I'll teach you how to kill. Simple."

"You want to use me."

"Yes, and feel free to use me back."

She looked him up and down. "I don't trust you."

"That makes you stronger. I like that. If you're strong, you'll stand a chance against those you want to kill."

"How do you know who I want to kill?"

He smiled, and his red eyes sparked with something strange. "I told you, we share common enemies."

"Did they kill your parents, too?"

He chuckled. "No, but they killed my children."

"Why?"

He crouched and looked her in the eyes. "You're not ready for the reason why they kill. Let's keep it at that. When you're ready, I'll tell you."

She nodded.

"You have to keep this from Keymaster."

"Why? Are you his enemy? You can't use me to harm him."

"You're a smart kid," he said. "I have no intention of killing Keymaster. But he has to focus on making keys. That's his job. So why don't we let him focus on that?"

"You have to promise no harm will come to Keymaster."

"I can promise not to harm him. But I can't control others' intentions. And there are many others who want him dead, little child. He'll be dead one day. He can't protect you forever. So you'd better get some real training. What do you say?"

She looked up at him, then she nodded. She would learn the necessary skills from him. She would figure out the next step later.

CHAPTER 8

Caedmon picked himself up from the floor. It felt as if he had been struck by lightning. Not that he'd ever been struck before, nor did he want to know how it really felt. Pukak moved quite quickly for an old man. Caedmon was sure he could take him down, even in his ordinary human body, but he wasn't going to fight an old man.

Caedmon wiped the blood from his cut lip. "You can't beat someone up for no reason," he said. "A mage has a code of conduct, does he not?"

Ben walked into the room and glared at Caedmon.

"Ben said you put light into Alyna," Pukak growled. "I know you're not a mage. You're a creature. But what exactly are you? Why are you infiltrating Amaraq?"

Caedmon rubbed at his jaw. "So that's what this is about?" He chuckled. "I'm disappointed in Amaraq." He tapped his wrist unit. "I resuscitated Alyna with a special LeBlanc technology. Yes, it does have a kind of electric current. When I performed CPR on her, she stopped breathing. You're suggesting I should have stood there and watched her die?"

"It was magic!" Ben growled.

"It's advanced technology, not magic."

"Let me see!" Pukak reached his hand out.

There was no way Caedmon was going to let anyone touch his wrist unit, the crucial piece of technology that connected him with Eudaiz. Not only it was his only way back, but it also carried critical information about his make along with a lot of Eudaizian technology.

He had used his eudqi to resuscitate Alyna. He'd switched on his silver blood special energy and pumped it into her. Ben would have seen his palm glowing when he performed the procedure, but he wouldn't have seen the dematerialized creature that had attacked her. Human eyes couldn't detect dematerialized forms.

"It's patented technology. I can't let you handle it."

"I only want to look at it. You think an old man like me could steal your technology?"

"I can't let anyone touch it. It's that simple. If you don't want our business, then I'll go." He walked toward the door, but Ben stopped him.

Pukak turned toward him. "You want our secrets. I can't let you go."

Caedmon chuckled. "Look, it's blatantly obvious that you are in financial ruin. I can walk out of here and forget about Amaraq in no time. This isn't a big deal to the LeBlancs."

Ben threw a punch at his abdomen. Caedmon saw it coming, and he could have stopped the hit, but he didn't. *Be human!* he reminded himself. He didn't have his special energy on, but even with his human body, he was a lot faster and stronger than an ordinary human like Ben—if Ben wasn't a mage.

But judging from the punch, Ben was only human.

Caedmon heaved and clutched at his stomach. No matter how strong he was, a punch in full force still hurt.

Ben grabbed Caedmon's collar and shoved him against the wall. "Fight back. Show me what you've got. Show me you have super power."

"If I had super power, I'd break you in half right now."

Ben punched him again, but this time, Caedmon grabbed his fist. "I'm not trained in martial arts like you, but I don't care for being bullied. I offered financial help.

If you don't want it, then let me go." He pushed Ben away. Ben looked at Pukak.

"Let him go. I have to see to Alyna now," Pukak said.

"Pukak, he spied on us! I'm telling you he's something else. No one without training can block my punch—"

Caedmon punched Ben in the face, sending him reeling backward. "Violence needs no training. Now, that's just a taste of it. Don't piss me off, Ben." Then he kicked the door open and walked out.

On the street, a few blocks away from Alyna's place, Caedmon turned onto a quiet corner and turned on his wrist unit. Lorcan appeared on the screen.

"You didn't even give me enough time to drink a glass of water before you called back, Caedmon."

"The plan has changed, Uncle Lorcan. Amaraq just kicked me out."

"That's good. Get out of that mess, Caedmon. The key might not be with them."

"What do you mean?"

"You asked me to look into Ethesus, so I took a quick peek. Amaraq isn't a transformed version of the mage tribe that you and Sedna took the key from. They existed at the same time. So did Ethesus. The tribe you and Sedna worked with was the only one with pure and consistent energy. Amaraq and Ethesus were messy. If

Amaraq were a genuine mage operating group, someone at high rank in that group would have a connection with the multiverse. Same with Ethesus. So before you know who is who, and who is looking for what, get the hell out of there and give me some more time to dig deeper."

"Can you get me the list of those in Amaraq that might have shady connections?"

"Yes, but it'll take some time. And why do you care, Caedmon? You've been there for, what, two seconds? Get the hell out of there."

"I'll see what I can do."

"Don't do anything silly, son. Your father might be bed-bound for a week, but nothing can stop me from alerting your extensive family in Eudaiz and a series of kick-ass commanders to drag your ass back where you belong."

"Understood." He heard a noise and footsteps from just around the corner. "I've got to go." As soon as he turned the communicator off, Ben stepped out with a dozen men.

"Pukak said to let you leave, but he didn't tell me not to beat you up. No one lays a punch on me and walks away intact."

"I'm sorry I hurt your ego. But you attacked me first."

"You asked for it. I know what you did for Alyna had nothing to do with technology. I'm not a mage, but I work with enough supernatural people to be able tell the difference."

Caedmon smiled. "Even Pukak can't tell. So do you mean you work with higher caliber supernatural people, perhaps crossing between Amaraq and Ethesus camps?"

"Bullshit. Get him." Ben signaled, and the dozen men behind him charged at Caedmon.

CHAPTER 10

Alyna whirled around, grabbed her boots, and slid them on.

"Can you slow down, Alyna? You just got up on your feet." Pukak looked at her in disapproval.

"Ben will hurt Caedmon. I'm sure of it."

"Alyna, Caedmon isn't exactly defenseless."

"But you said Caedmon punched Ben in the face."

"Yes."

"A man with crushed ego is dangerous. Ben hurts people, not the other way around. That's how he operates. Caedmon can throw a few punches, but he's just a corporate guy. I doubt he has any combat training."

Pukak chuckled. "You should see how he punches."

"What do you mean?"

"Nothing. Maybe he's just talented."

Alyna rushed out of the house and darted around the corner and down a dark street that led to the main road. If Caedmon wanted to get transport back to his quarter, he would have headed that way.

***

Caedmon smiled at Ben. He would teach this human and his petty ego a lesson to remember. As the group of twelve charged at Caedmon, he switched his eudqi on. The super energy enhanced his natural agility and gave him incredible speed and strength. That was all he needed with this group of humans.

Soon, the group of men were crawling on the ground, moaning. They slowly got up but didn't dare charge again. Caedmon looked straight at Ben, cocking an eyebrow. The other men looked at Ben, too. Ben had no choice but to run at Caedmon.

In a swift move, Caedmon knocked him to the ground. He made sure he had total control of his strength. He didn't want to break the guy's neck.

Then, because his super power was on and his senses were super sensitive, he heard breathing and movement from Alyna. She was rushing toward him.

He immediately switched off his super power.

At the same time, Ben pushed himself up from the ground and charged at him again. They fought, exchanging blow for blow.

The other men could see the changes in the synergy of the fight.

"Get him, you cowards!" Ben shouted at them.

They all rushed at Caedmon at the same time. What followed was a sea of fists, legs, and elbows. All Caedmon was worried about was protecting his wrist unit. In the worst-case scenario, he could just open a portal and leave, but without the wrist unit, he'd be stranded on Earth.

"Stop! Stop all of you!"

It was Alyna's voice. The stream of punches and kicks stopped. He pushed the man standing next to him aside and walked away.

"Thirteen of you against one?" Alyna said.

"You should have seen him before," Ben said.

"Yes, I heard. He punched you in the face, didn't he? You embarrass me, Ben. Now go. All of you."

Caedmon heard the footsteps of the retreating men and then Alyna's footsteps, following him.

His injuries hurt. All he needed was to turn on his eudqi. The healing process would start instantly, and he would be in perfect condition in no time. But he couldn't do that in front of Alyna or any other human. He needed the privacy of the unit where he was staying.

He felt Alyna's hand touching his shoulder. She turned him around. "This looks really bad, Caedmon. I have to take you to a medical center. Our clinic is closer, and they'd do a good job, but I don't think you'd like it. Please let me take you to the medical center."

"I just need to be left alone. Thank you." He kept walking—or maybe he was passing out? He could feel that a couple of his ribs were broken. He was hurting badly and needed to heal them as soon as possible.

He felt Alyna's arm around his waist. She was a lot stronger than he expected. "If you don't want to go to the medical center, fine," she said. "But I have to at least get you home safely. You owe me, remember?"

"Excuse me?"

"When you unclasped my bra, you said I could beat you up if I wanted to."

"That was rhetorical."

"But I took it literally. Obviously, I don't want to beat you up. But I do want to take you home."

"Fine," he muttered. He tried to be as unfriendly as he could, but it didn't deter her. He'd have to play along. They walked for one more block and were about to get to the main road when they heard stealthy footsteps. He recognized them. They weren't the footsteps of thugs from street gangs. They were the stealthy steps of well-trained mercenaries.

Alyna left him leaning against a wall and put her hands on her two guns.

"Seriously, Alyna?"

"It's Ethesus. And yes, I'm very serious."

"You can't just kill people on the street."

"It's kill or be killed, Caedmon. I don't know about you, but I prefer the former. I want you to get down as low as you can."

"No."

"Caedmon! There's no room for ego here. I'm the one with the guns."

"I can use one of yours."

"Have you ever fired a gun before?"

"I know how to pull a trigger."

She nodded and reluctantly gave him one of her two guns.

While she was busy surveying the surrounding area, he switched his eudqi on. He could feel the healing energy surging through his body, fixing his broken ribs. But he stopped the process at ninety percent, leaving all his external injuries as they were.

They walked along a narrow street with high fences on either side. He could see that while Alyna might be lethal at one-on-one fighting, she had no combat training at all.

They were in the worst possible position for an ambush. He turned his eudqi totally off, but with his human eyes and ears, he could still see the movement of the mercenaries on the roofs of the houses along the narrow street.

He could gun down a few, but he would need to save the eudqi for healing purposes because he was sure he would suffer more injuries. He wasn't worried about himself but was concerned for Alyna. As far as he knew, she was human and had no special healing power. If she was shot, she might die.

He had no problem protecting himself. But he had no confidence that he could protect Alyna as well.

As he predicted, several mercenaries emerged at the top of the high fence. Judging by their skilled movements, he figured they must be at the top of the pay rank in the multiverse.

"They aren't Ethesus," Alyna whispered.

CHAPTER 11

Alyna didn't like what she was thinking. The movements of the assailants told her they weren't Ethesus, but they weren't ordinary fighters, either. She had nothing that anyone on Earth could possibly want—no money, no possessions—and she wasn't exactly an important person.

She was a kick-ass fighter, however, and because of that, they would get nothing at all for fighting her except injuries–some of which might be fatal.

Whatever they wanted must have to do with Caedmon. She cursed herself for not having thought about this before. With his background, he was an attractive target for any scumbag looking for money, power, or anything Caedmon's family could provide. In this stretch of town, people would kill for a simple lunch credit. The only thing that comforted her now was that if her prediction was right, and someone went after Caedmon for money, then at least they wouldn't harm him.

Six mercenaries jumped from the high fence, landing softly like feathers floating to the ground. They didn't pull out weapons. She stepped in front of Caedmon. She could sense his movement behind her as he attempted to get equal ground with her, so she sidestepped and blocked his way. He seemed to get the hint and stopped trying.

"You're not locals. What do you want?" Alyna asked.

The shortest of the six to the far left answered. "Caedmon LeBlanc," he said.

"He's Amaraq's client, under my protection. So the answer is no, you can't have him."

The short man chuckled. "You must be Alyna McCabe."

"I hope I have a good reputation in the South. Now that I have declined your request, we would like to go, preferably in peace."

"What exactly do you want from me?" Caedmon asked.

The short man smirked, and his green eyes flashed an unusual shade. "Your wrist unit," he said. "But it won't work without you, so we need the whole package."

"Well, I'll give you my coat. It's worth much more. And it works without me."

Alyna wanted to chuckle, but she figured it would probably be a bad idea, so she maintained a poker face. The short man opened his mouth and was about to respond when Alyna felt the brush of Caedmon's arm against her side. She knew what he was doing, but it happened so fast it surprised her.

Caedmon gunned down the short man before he could utter a response.

She followed suit with the other men. It all happened so quickly there was no time to think. For her, it was just muscle memory from years of training. She didn't know what sort of training Caedmon had had, but he was extremely fast and accurate. She shot two men on the far right and threw a knife into a third to her left. Her left hand was working much better than her right because of the injury she'd suffered in a fight with an Ethesus supreme fighter the other week. The knife entered the temple of the assailant, and he was no longer part of the equation. Only one of the shots she had fired was lethal.

She pushed Caedmon, and they both jumped behind a barrel of industrial waste along the side of the road, but the path was narrow and the bin not large enough to cover them completely.

"Three left, one of them injured. Can you handle the injured one?" Caedmon asked.

She didn't take it as an insult, but his question did hurt her ego. She said nothing but pointed her gun and fired without looking. The injured man she had shot before dropped in midair as he tried to leap over the bin at them.

"Second time, not too lucky," she muttered and charged out from behind the bin.

The other two were about to attack when they saw her. She lowered her gun. "Me against two of you. What do you say?"

She knew mercenaries. They essentially did what she did for a living. The difference was that she was paid to protect people, and they were paid to cause harm. Either way, they all had a code of conduct. She had issued them a challenge, and they had no choice but to take it.

As she predicted, they both lowered their guns and charged at her.

She took them on. They exchanged strikes, blow for blow. Although she didn't recognize their style of martial arts, she had to admit they were good.

She scored several blows to their heads and bodies. If it had been a performance fight at her club, she would have been declared the winner. But this wasn't a stage fight. After suffering several hits, they backed up against the wall. She knew their intentions—they were paid predators after all.

Both of them had their hands on their guns.

Her reaction was again pure muscle memory. She pulled her gun with her left hand and fired at the man on the left. Caedmon had already moved to stand by her right-hand side, and he shot the man on the right–her weak side.

As the mercenaries fell to the ground, she looked up at Caedmon. Tall. Calm. Dark hair. Striking gray eyes. He looked magnificent, like a warrior in some ancient movie about the time before the Great War.

She holstered her gun. He gave her back the other.

"No, you keep it," she said.

He nodded and smiled, wincing a bit when he tried to tuck the gun into his belt.

She realized that the few-thousand-credit outfits he'd been wearing weren't designed to carry weapons. "Just put it here," she said and took the gun and slid it into his jacket pocket. "The safety's on, so it won't discharge involuntarily. But you're not exactly shabby at handling a gun, so I guess you know the basics."

Caedmon nodded and absently moved his hand to his side. She could only hope her men had left no marks on his elegant body. She could only hope there were no severe internal injuries.

"What hurts?" she asked.

"Huh?"

"Apart from the external bruises I can see, do you have any internal injuries caused by my men? If so, I'll take you to the medical clinic."

"No, it's nothing. Just some scratches. What are we going to do with these bodies?"

"Leave them. The trucks will get them in the morning."

"You mean the garbage trucks?"

"Kind of, but these pick up industrial waste. They're paid to collect both private and industrial waste."

"But these are humans. And they're dead. Won't people ask questions?"

"Who would ask? And ask what?" She had no idea what he was talking about. In her town, if people didn't protect themselves, they'd be killed. When humans died, they became waste—literally. If the death happened inside the household, it was private waste. But this was a public footpath, so it was considered industrial waste.

He looked baffled, and she shrugged. "Let's get you home," she said.

He nodded and strode ahead. She followed, still not understanding his concern about the waste issue.

Suddenly, there was a sound. It sounded like metal bars scraping against each other. And there were the strange noises of things communicating with each other in a language she didn't know. She had no idea what it was she was hearing, but she was sure it wasn't human.

CHAPTER 12

Bang.

The Keymaster was so startled by the loud noise that he almost fell off his chair.

Bang.

"That's enough, child!"

Bang. Bang. Bang.

He left the workshop where he was working on the stone for the Scorpio key and went to the backyard to see what she was up to. The Thunder Child was building something that looked like a gallows.

"Planning to hang some criminals?" he asked.

She giggled. "No, Keymaster. This is so you can hang a blade to cut stone. Given that you're having such difficulty carving the bloodstone…"

"Child, you don't have to worry about that. It's my job to cut the bloodstone. I've done this for hundreds of years. All stones are different. And yes, this bloodstone is stubborn. But there's no stone I can't cut."

"I know, but this machine will give you some assistance. Watch…" She pulled a lever, and a steel blade came crashing down from above with incredible force, slamming into the stone base below it.

Keymaster's head rang with the sound, which bounced from his left ear to his right ear and then back around his head.

"Child, don't do that. Why don't you leave the key-making business to me? You're still young. Go pick some flowers."

"Can I go into the woods?"

"Hmmm…"

She reached for the lever again.

"Okay, sure," he said quickly. "You can play by the woods. But be sure to come home before dark."

She grinned. "Yes, Keymaster."

"What do I always tell you?"

"Don't play with creatures in the woods, don't talk to strangers, and don't engage in eye contact with any creature from the magical world. If anything attacks, don't run. Turn on the safety lock, and call for Keymaster," she said solemnly.

"Very good. Where is your safety lock?"

She pushed aside the little cloak he had made her to show him the lock underneath.

He smiled. "Go play."

She grinned, and then her tiny shadow ran a zigzag all the way up the hill toward the wedge of woods she liked.

He returned to his studio.

"Oh no!"

The shard of bloodstone he had worked on had returned to its original shape.

CHAPTER 13

Caedmon went back to the foyer of the building where he was staying. The sight of Alyna standing next to a grand marble column reminded him of his wife, Sedna. The flashback hit him unexpectedly, and he was totally unprepared for it. He knew what his physical reaction would be with such an emotional hit. Weeping in public was unacceptable in any universe, so he immediately turned away and hurried into a nearby restroom.

He had met Sedna at a museum in London where there was an exhibition of Eskimo history and artifacts.

She was a high-end antique buyer, and he was researching the cultural development of Eskimo tribes. At least that was his cover. He needed to obtain the Scorpio key, and she was the upcoming leader of the mage tribe that held the key. But their relationship wasn't all a ploy. They loved each other, and before he knew it, they were married.

He felt the heat of the blast again as if it exploded in his mind right now–the blast that had robbed him of his family.

He didn't know what had happened, but before he knew it, security had entered the bathroom. When he came to his senses, he saw that the mirror in front of him was shattered, and there was blood all over his hands.

He was angry. The heat rising inside him wasn't the heat from the blast that had killed Sedna but heat from the urge to seek vengeance. He had never experienced this before. The heat consumed him. Waves of pain pounded and echoed in his head. Blood threatened to erupt from his veins. His vision blurred. He could hear Sedna screaming in agony, but he knew that even if she were in excruciating pain, she would never utter a sound.

He hated. The word *hate* had never been in his vocabulary. His father had always said he wasn't capable of hate. Even his twin sister did better than he in expressing negative emotions. That was why his father said he could never be a true human—because he didn't know how to express and control his emotions.

But the hate invaded his mind now, and it totally took him over. He couldn't control his emotions, and the rage burst from him like a volcano.

But once it was out, he felt peace.   The haze of strange visions and pain and the images of blood and gore cleared a bit, revealing the room he was in. Things cleared enough for him to see that the blood and gore wasn't just a part of his visions. It was real. It was as if the two guards who had grabbed him from behind had exploded into pieces.

From the corner of his eye, he saw Alyna step through the door. He looked at his shaky hands, bloody from cuts from the broken glass of the mirror. Then he looked at her. "I...I don't know what happened," he said.

She stepped out of the room and glanced down the corridor. Then she pulled him outside and slammed the door closed.

"Where's your compartment?" she asked.

He pulled out his key card and gave it to her. It glowed with a map of the building and identified the desired compartment.

"Let's go," she said and pushed him along the corridor, following the shiny arrow on the key card. "Like I told you before, the two dead guards are now just domestic waste. Nobody will question the bodies. But the way in which they died will be questioned. You have to give me an explanation for this. But first, let's get you cleaned up."

They stood in front of his compartment. She swiped the key and pushed the door open. She pushed him down onto the sofa in the living wing then went into the bathroom to get some wet towels, water, and a first-aid kit.

When she came back to the living room, his head was clearer.

"Do you think my energy caused the two guards to explode?"

She pulled a footstool over, sat opposite him, and started cleaning the blood from his hands and shirt.

He looked at his shirt. "It's probably not worth cleaning this." He took it off and caught her glancing at the bruises from the fight with her men. He was glad he had repaired ninety percent of the broken ribs. Otherwise, he wouldn't have been able to keep his face impassive while she cleaned him up.

"It didn't hurt," he said.

She arched an eyebrow. "Is that so? What about this?" she said and pushed her palm right at the spot of his broken ribs.

He winced.

"I won't force you to go to our medical clinic, especially if you aren't exactly human. They wouldn't care for that. But you have to get this fixed at a medical center—"

There was a knock on the door.

She stopped talking, went to the door, and looked at the security monitor. "There's a Barbie here looking for you."

"Excuse me?"

"A stunning blonde is looking for you."

"I don't know who that would be."

Alyna looked into the monitor. "Who's there?"

"Leanne. I'm Caedmon's executive secretary. Here are my credentials."

Alyna looked at the screen then at Caedmon. He nodded. Alyna unlocked the door.

Leanne stepped into the room like a breath of fresh air, and she zeroed right in on the injuries to Caedmon's upper body.

"I knew it. I knew this would happen when I found out that Mr. Tann advised you to go to the North side." She rushed over and shuffled through the medical kit.

"It's all right, Leanne. It was just an accident."

Alyna approached and pushed Leanne's hands away. "Don't chip your nails, Leanne. I'm Alyna by the way. I'm the head of security at Amaraq. And I apologize…Caedmon's injuries were a misunderstanding."

"Of course. It was truly a misunderstanding, Alyna. I'm new in town, and things are a little confusing for me. Sometimes things aren't what they appear to be," he said, locking eyes with Alyna. He knew she had questions about the incident in the restroom, but he didn't have any good answers for her.

Alyna nodded. "All right, get some rest, Caedmon. I'll see you again some other time if you're still interested in our business after this." She nodded a goodbye and left.

Leanne grabbed a towel and got down on all fours to mop up the muddy shoeprints Alyna had left on the carpet and the floor.

"You don't have to do this, Leanne." Caedmon crouched to pull her up from the floor.

"No, no…don't touch me. I've just touched the dirty floor, and you have open wounds."

"It's just a few scratches. No big deal."

"I don't know how developed the LeBlanc's pharmaceutical products are in Mid-land London, but here, the species of bacteria and virus have mutated so drastically that there would be no cure if you were infected."

"Okay, I'll try to stay clear of all sources of possible infection."

She nodded. "It's normally fine if you're healthy, fit, and strong. But when you're injured, or your body is weakened for some reason, you have to be careful."

"Can I ask you a question? You don't have to answer if you don't want to."

"Sure, anything."

"How open are people here to creatures that aren't…human?"

"You mean the supernatural?"

He nodded cautiously.

"We all know that supernaturals live among us. They come and go from different places. But on Earth, humans are the majority. People don't like to mix with supernaturals. I can't speak for others, but if I see a vampire, and he doesn't want to stick his fangs in my neck, I could care less that he exists. But normal people don't like them. So if you know any supernaturals, tell them to be careful."

"Thank you."

"For what?"

"For dropping by. For checking on me."

"It's my job." She smiled. "Alyna likes you."

Caedmon chucked. "She considers me her responsibility. Or maybe worse, a liability."

"Amaraq is a mage operating organization. You know that, right?"

He nodded.

"You asked if humans discriminated against supernaturals. The answer is yes. But mages don't trust humans or any other creatures. So the line between who is discriminating against whom is very thin."

CHAPTER 14

Alyna approached the building complex. Her compartment was on the ground floor at the far back corner. She had chosen the location because of its backyard with privacy for her outdoor martial arts practice and the basement which was convenient for her shooting practice. What had happened with Caedmon was disconcerting. She could get past the look in Caedmon's eyes. The rage. She knew about such emotions. She herself had a temper, and it sometimes scared off the men around her.

But what she had seen in Caedmon's eyes was the true definition of rage. It was something she'd never seen before in her life. It was another mystery to which she'd need to find answers. And that was on top of the shadow that had tried to kill her at Tony's place. What kind of supernatural creature was that? And why did it want to kill her?

She saw a shadow at the corner of her yard next to the fence. She'd had a hell of a day and needed nothing less than to release her frustration on a random trespasser.

"Hey!" she shouted and charged at the shadow.

"Please don't hurt me."

"Sam? Now I really have to hurt you. You didn't show up at the club like you promised." She playfully shoved the shoulder of the teenager she had helped the other day with a couple of credit tokens.

"I didn't promise anything. You asked me to go. I'm here to give you back your credits."

He opened his palm, revealing two shiny credit tokens.

"Did you steal those?"

He shook his head. "No, but I didn't earn them, either. Ben gave them to me and asked me to spy on you, so I quit. What sort of club pays members to spy on their leader?"

"Ben Zuric?"

"Yes. When I told him you sent me, he asked me to report to him what you've been up to. He thinks we're close. Before we had a chance to finish the conversation, he got an emergency call. Something about a dead body. Anyway, I left."

"First, I am highly ranked in Amaraq, but I'm not their leader. Pukak is. Second, I know Ben. He wouldn't betray me. Until I have hard evidence, I'm not going to draw any conclusions. Maybe he just wants to know which club I'll be auditing next so he can prepare for it. There's nothing wrong with that. Again, I advise you to come back. As for the credits, keep them. They're yours, whether you join Amaraq or not. But living in this day and age, I strongly recommend you try to protect yourself. If you come back, the club door is always open for you."

She turned to go inside.

"What's the catch, Alyna?" Sam asked from behind her.

"You owe me a favor."

He nodded. "I can live with that. Oh…hey…"

Alyna turned around and saw Sam approaching a cat sitting in the dark next to a trash can. He approached the cat slowly, reaching his hand out. The cat sniffed then licked his hand. He scratched the cat under its jaw. The cat purred audibly.

She approached to join him, but when she got close, the cat stopped purring. It stared at her with two glowing green eyes.

"Hello, beautiful," she said.

The cat left Sam and approached her. It emerged from the shadows, and she could now see its long, gray fur in the dim streetlights. It was truly beautiful.

"Look at your tail," Sam said and was about to stroke the cat's tail, which had an unusual T-shape at the end.

"No, Sam, cats don't like you to stroke their tails."

The cat approached her, and it sat down in front of her and stared.

Sam chuckled. "If you want to enter a staring competition with Alyna, you will lose, cat! Why don't you come with me? I have one credit left. I can share half of it with you and buy you a can of processed fish. How does that sound?"

It kept looking at Alyna and ignored Sam's questions.

Alright, you're challenging me! she thought. Her inner voice screamed at her to drop the idea, but she wasn't the kind to obey orders easily. So she did what she didn't think she would ever be capable of doing again. She hummed the tune of the lullaby her mother used to sing to her when she was younger. As soon as she started, the cat stood up and walked slowly around her.

Next, she started softly singing the words. As soon as she did so, the cat bit her finger lightly. She continued singing. The cat bit harder.

"Don't do that, naughty cat," Sam said and reached over to pull the cat away. The cat turned around and hissed at him. Its eyes sparked as if they would shoot fire. Sam recoiled.

Alyna stopped singing.

The cat cast a glance at her and then at Sam. Then it turned around and walked away.

Sam looked at her. "Hey, what's up? I'm going to get you another cat. Don't worry. There are plenty of them around town, especially on the back streets." Sam's voice was a bit shaky.

She realized she was crying and wiped away the tears.

"I mean, it was a cute cat, but it bit you. I can find you another one, preferably one with a gentler nature."

"You can't replace him."

Sam shrugged. "I don't see anything special about that cat."

"His name is Lazi. He has long gray fur, a crooked tail, and he hates that lullaby. He would bite, scratch, and meow until my mother stopped singing."

"Oh, so that's *your* cat. Don't worry then. I'll get him back for you."

"Don't worry, Sam. You won't be able to find him."

"Why not? He's unusual. I could easily tell him apart from other cats. What's the problem, Alyna?"

"When I was a teenager, my parents died in a car accident. Lazi died in that car crash, too."

CHAPTER 15

Caedmon awoke to the sound of a message coming through on his wrist unit. He vaguely remembered seeing Leanne to the door then rushing back into the room to turn on his eudqi and heal his injuries, leaving some of the cuts and bruises that could obviously not heal themselves overnight untouched to avoid suspicion. After that, he'd crashed on the bed for hours.

He initiated the large screen mode of the wrist unit, and a floating screen appeared in the air. On it was Lorcan, who frowned at his visible wounds.

"Uncle Lorcan! Long story," he said, gesturing at his injuries, "but they're just minor flesh wounds. What have you got for me?"

"Good news or bad news first?"

"Good news, please."

"Because—out of the goodness of your heart—you expressed concern about Amaraq's welfare, I dug around a bit. I found some possible connections. It seems there are tensions between Amaraq and Ethesus regarding their businesses and their spiritual territories."

"Spiritual practices have a territory?"

Lorcan chuckled. "Apparently they do. Normal humans need some kind of structure and guidance in their lives to operate together as a functioning society. When no tangible government-established authority exists, humans turn to a higher power, a spiritual belief. It might be in the form of religion, or it could be just a belief in righteousness. Whatever it is, the business competition between Amaraq and Ethesus is more than just a fight for financial territories—their spiritual practices are a large part of it as well. Humans need to believe in something to function."

"I was told last night that humans often discriminate against the supernaturals. On top of that, the supernaturals are territorial and discriminate among themselves. It sounds like the Great War made humans jump out of the frying pan into the fire."

"Yes, the Great War." Lorcan rolled his eyes. "Wiping out all governments and authorities gave Earth a spiritually barbarian society…"

"And the links to Amaraq are?"

"Oh, sorry. I got sidetracked," Lorcan said with a chuckle. "There's a Ben Zuric in the Amaraq who has a questionable background. Records show he joined via a recommendation by Alyna McCabe. But the Zurics are Ethesus people, meaning Ben's family has connections with the Ethesus. Family matters are complicated, but in terms of spiritual beliefs, it's rare that they swing between the two extremes."

"Amaraq has a client who died yesterday, and they suspect his death was due to spiritual conflicts between family members."

Lorcan nodded. "I don't know what sort of records Amaraq has on Ben Zuric or what sort of person he is. But if you're looking for people with shady connections, I'd start with him."

"All right, I'll look into it. Thanks, Uncle Lorcan. And by the way, there was a group of top-grade mercenaries sent after me yesterday."

Lorcan arched an eyebrow. "That would have to do with the bad news I have for you. There's an alert in the system. Someone tried to do a search of your records in the LeBlanc's database. It was an amateur attempt, of course, because they didn't have access, and they left traces of their search. But someone at the branch you're working with is either questioning your cover or wants to leverage it for profits. Either way, the enemy is in your own backyard."

"I have an idea of who it might be…"

Caedmon felt a sudden rush of cold air behind him. He remembered that he still had his eudqi on since starting the healing process last night, so his senses were ultra-sharp.

"I have something to show you," he said to Lorcan and turned around as if getting something for him.

He switched on his microchip and scanned the room. The microchip eyes detected the form of a creature made of black particles. It stood on two legs and looked like a werewolf, but it had horns. The particle form was blurry. He didn't know what it was, but he knew it could dematerialize. It could be the creature that had attacked Alyna earlier.

It stood still as he nonchalantly moved toward it. It was a truly dematerialized creature. He walked right through it as he moved to the other side of the room. He predicted it would be able to will enough force to kill humans without having to rematerialize. That was how it had attacked Alyna and possibly killed her client. But it couldn't attack him in its dematerialized form because he was also a creature from the multiverse. Whether *he* could attack and kill a dematerialized creature, he had no idea.

His strongest talent was to create light blades— they were like lightning that could slice through any solid surface. He could cause a small earthquake or cut off a piece of arctic ice. But his blades weren't suitable for use in confined spaces. He could certainly swing a dagger at the creature or shoot it with his laser gun, but if his attempts failed to kill the creature, it would be alerted that he could see it in its dematerialized form.

He recalled his experience last night in the bathroom when the surge of heat and energy from his anger had blown up the two guards. Maybe he could use that against the creature. If it didn't work, at least his attempt wouldn't be too obvious.

He concentrated, gathered his thoughts, summoned his rage, and sent a blast of heat toward the creature. The wave of fiery torridity blanketed it.

He heard a roar.

It worked!

The creature staggered and materialized, becoming semitransparent. He sent another heatwave. It roared again and turned to run. He blasted one more time. He wasn't sure he could grab the creature, but he wanted to make sure it didn't get away. It looked as if it was about to jump into a dimensional gateway, so he sent one more strong blast. The blast was too strong—it sucked a large part of his energy out with it.

But the creature roared louder and completely materialized. It was a nine-foot-tall werewolf lookalike with horns. As if that wasn't unusual enough, it was made of ice. And the ice was cracking and melting under the impact of the heatwaves.

Now it had materialized completely. It could attack him.

Because he was losing so much energy, Caedmon wasn't sure he had the strength to go up against this creature. When it charged at him and made contact, he did what he had done last night to the two guards—he pumped his rage into it.

The ice creature exploded into thousands of pieces of ice which quickly evaporated.

On the ground lay a single palm-sized shard of red ice. It looked like frozen blood.

CHAPTER 16

Ben pushed open the door of the fight club. He had been with this club for a long time, and he knew his way around. Countless times, he had asked himself why he stayed in one place for so long. Every single time, the answer was Alyna. He didn't like that answer.

He had been a rogue before she'd introduced him to the club. And she had been more of a rogue than he was. *Did anyone question her background before she joined Amaraq?* he wondered. Probably not, because she was at the highest rank, just under Pukak.

He would never forget the look on her face when she found him at the dumpster years ago. They'd both been teenagers at the time, but Alyna had already achieved a decent rank in Amaraq. People told him she had climbed up the ladder quickly though she had joined not long before he had. She had claimed her rank purely by her talent. It had taken him much longer to make progress within Amaraq.

Ben had worked for this fight club for a long time under Tomkin, a guy he didn't have much respect for and didn't consider to be highly talented. As far as he was concerned, Tomkin was a spineless sucker. Before he knew it, time had passed, and he'd worked for Amaraq for far too long. He was going nowhere in this so-called career.

He could move to the South. Amaraq had no idea how many times he had turned down offers there just to stay put and help them here in the North. But if his loyalty wasn't appreciated, he should just go. If he didn't take care of himself, nobody else would, that was for sure.

In this society, it was either kill or be killed. Wasn't that what Alyna had always told him? He was merely protecting himself and working toward his future. That's what everyone did, right? Feeling somewhat comfortable with his reasoning, he ran his hand under the doormat where he knew Tomkin hid the key whenever he went out of town on Amaraq business.

Ben knew his way around well enough inside the club. He could work there all night without the need for a light. He knew that on his right was a large fighting platform where they organized competitions and recruited followers for the private security business. There were several surveillance cameras in that area. Although they used an ancient technology from the middle of the third millennium, it still recorded data. He didn't want his face to show up as a suspected thief.

He stayed as far to the left as possible. There wasn't much surveillance on that side. There was a medical center, some changing rooms and bathrooms, and a couple of supporting offices. He used the key, sneaked into an office, and shuffled through the filing cabinets.

There it was—the file on Alyna. He pulled the folder out, flipped quickly through the documents inside, and cursed. This was a file on her training and achievements in martial arts. Not what he was looking for.

"Idiot!" he cursed himself. The file must be in Pukak's office—or whatever he called the dump he used as the medical clinic. He didn't have much time left, so he left the fight club and headed toward the clinic.

All was dark from the outside, meaning Pukak had left. Ben hugged the side wall, took a couple of running steps for momentum, then jumped on top of a trash can and leaped onto the roof.

Who in this day and age used tiles on the roof of a house? he wondered.

He pulled off a bit of the roof tile and peeked into Pukak's office. It was empty. Holding onto the edge of the roof, Ben lowered himself to the ground and sneaked inside the clinic. Stepping over piles of papers and jars and buckets of god knows what kinds of medicine, Ben reached the filing cabinet. He pulled a drawer open, shuffled through the folders, and found Alyna's file. He pulled it out.

Suddenly the room lit up. In the doorway stood Alyna, Pukak, and Caedmon.

Ben slammed the cabinet drawer closed. "It isn't what it looks like!" he said.

"So what should it look like, apart from you being a traitor?" Pukak asked.

"No!" He saw the look of disappointment in Alyna's eyes. "No, I can explain."

"Sure you can. But it had better be something other than the fact that your family is with Ethesus, because I've already told them that," Caedmon said.

"Bastard!" Ben leaped on top of the table and jumped from it over to Caedmon. Alyna pushed

Caedmon aside and caught Ben midair with a kick, sending him crashing to the floor. She pulled him up by the collar and threw him against the wall.

"I'm not fighting you, Alyna."

She kicked him in his abdomen. "That's for lying to me and telling me your family was dead when I picked you up at the dumpster."

He fell to the ground and heaved.

She pulled him up again and punched him in the face. "And that's for never telling me about your connection to Ethesus, even when you know how concerned we are about them."

He rubbed his jaw. He knew Alyna had no tolerance for betrayal—a few more punches from her would be lethal. He could explain, but he didn't have a leg to stand on right now. All the evidence was pointing toward him.

He could only curse his stupidity. But he refused to go down that easily. He pulled a knife out, but before he could throw it, Alyna caught it by the blade. Blood seeped out between her fingers as she looked at him.

He knew the pain of being betrayed was a lot more difficult for her to handle than the physical pain caused by the knife. He let go of the knife.

"This," she said, "is for betraying Amaraq." She swung her fist at his temple, and his whole world went black.

CHAPTER 17

Caedmon lowered himself from the roof of the fight club where they were keeping Ben. His eudqi was turned on to enhance his movements and senses. The club had been quiet since training hours ended, but there were a couple of guards at the front and about five of them inside.

He had encountered Amaraq's guards before and knew they were trained fighters. If they had been working with Ben previously and believed in his innocence, they might be upset to see him imprisoned.

Would they break him out? Caedmon wasn't sure. He knew he had to get to Ben first to get some answers.

On the fighting square, he saw a man come out to check on security. It must be Tomkin, the head of this fight club. He'd been away when Ben broke in. There was nothing glaringly alarming about Tomkin that he could tell from a quick scan. He was human and appeared to be normal, but his movements suggested he was quite agile and might be a good fighter. Caedmon waited as Tomkin finished his security check and returned to his office.

It seemed as if Tomkin was done for the day, so Caedmon left the fight club. He sneaked down to the basement where he'd seen Alyna put Ben in a cell.

Ben charged at the wall of steel bars, grabbed the bars and shook them in anger when he saw Caedmon walk in.

"You act as if you're innocent, Ben."

"I'm not innocent. But neither are you. You're here without the others, so you must want something they wouldn't approve of. Am I right?"

"I'm not interested in trading information with you or promising to get you out of lockup. And I'm not going to bother judging whether you're a good man or not. It's none of my business. But yes, I'm here for information."

"And you think I'm going to simply hand it over to you?"

"Yes, pretty much." Caedmon smiled at Ben. "You care for Alyna. If you're willing to betray the club, I believe you'd do it for her interests."

"What the fuck do you know?"

"There's no need for profanity. I won't even have to work hard to get information from you. It's written all over your face. But you resent the fact that Alyna doesn't read your signals."

"You can't speak for her."

"You're right. I can't. But it's blatantly obvious that Amaraq's interest is her top priority. I care for her, too, as a friend. But her interest in Amaraq will ultimately put her life in jeopardy. I'm here to tell you that, because she and Pukak won't listen to me."

Ben chuckled. "And you think they would listen to me now?"

"No, I don't think so. But you can tell me how to save Alyna. That is, if you care about her."

"I know when I'm being played." He walked to the bed in the cell and sat down. "Now if you'll excuse me, I need to get some sleep."

"I don't think you saw the thing that tried to kill Alyna at your client's place. But I did. It has some kind of connection with this." He pulled out a cooler and showed Ben the shard of red ice inside. The color drained from Ben's face.

"Where did you get that?"

"From the thing that tried to kill Alyna."

"That's not possible. It's supposed to protect her. Protect us."

Caedmon shrugged. "You don't have to tell me why you tried to find Alyna's file or why you think it will protect her. I know you recognize this ice from the artifact. You know it can't be faked. I'm telling you it will kill her, and I won't be around to resuscitate her like I did before."

"If you're thinking of accessing the Scorpio key, forget about it, unless you're a mage. I'm guessing you're not, though, because Pukak can tell if you're not one of them."

"Alyna isn't a mage, either. So you're saying that even at her rank, she doesn't have access to Scorpio key?"

"Only mage members have access. Not only that, they summon Scorpio key only once every century. So there's no way to tell if Alyna has access. And if that thing is going to kill her, you should tell her not to be at the summoning ceremony."

"When's that?"

"Next week. Look, I know you have an agenda, and I still don't trust you. But you showed me the ice, so

I do think you care. Let me tell you this—I don't think Alyna is a normal human. That's why I wanted to check her file. Rumor has it that Pukak rescued her from a major accident in which everyone died. She was lucky to survive. But the way in which she gained rank within Amaraq so quickly made me think they might be planning to use her for something spiritual."

"You don't mean they want to use her as sacrificial subject, do you?"

"What else could it be? They have the summoning ceremony coming up. All the supernatural creatures know about it. And let me tell you, they fight like mad dogs to host it. Amaraq has the right because they hold the Scorpio key. But it's really all a myth...hearsay. Because it occurs only every hundred years—well beyond a human lifespan—no human can verify it, and no one can talk about what happens at the ceremony. So if Alyna is human, she'll be safe because they wouldn't let her attend. That's why I'm looking for her file—to see what Amaraq has on her and whether they consider her to be a normal human."

"I know you can't just ask them, because if they saved Alyna just to sacrifice her at the summoning, they wouldn't admit it. But who else of high rank, apart from Pukak, has access to the Scorpio key?"

Ben shook his head. "I've never been to a mage meeting. I'm not sure if Alyna has or not. They're very exclusive. I know Pukak is a mage, and he runs the show when it comes to spiritual stuff."

"What about Ethesus?"

"What about them?"

"Well, you work for Amaraq. Don't you know Ethesus is your number one competitor?"

"I know it from a business standpoint. But as for the spiritual practice, I'm not involved at all."

"All right, I'll get some more information. If I find any evidence that they plan to use Alyna as a sacrificial lamb, I'll let her know. I'll put in a word for you as well."

Ben shook his head. "No need to speak for me!" Then he looked at Caedmon with a strange expression on his face. "They will soon find out."

"Find out what?"

Ben smiled. "That it has nothing do to with Alyna. But still, tell her to be careful. That's all I need you to do for me."

Caedmon nodded and left the basement.

CHAPTER 18

Alyna didn't know how long she had been standing in the alley next to her complex, staring at the trash cans. It was late in the morning. She was supposed to have finished her morning training and been headed to work by now. But she hadn't practiced today, and she hadn't yet gotten ready for work.

"The cat hasn't come back?" Sam asked from behind her.

She turned toward him. Sam was more mature than she would have thought for a teenager who picked pockets for a living. She guessed because he'd been living in tough conditions he was more street smart than most teens she had known. She shook her head.

"I told you, the cat died. It can't come back."

"Then what you are waiting here for?"

"An explanation. You touched the cat, right? It was real?"

Sam scratched his head. "Yes. So I guess the question is whether you're sure your cat was dead. Or whether you're sure *that* cat was your dead cat."

She shook her head. She really had no idea. "I need to look into this further. Can you keep this between you me?"

"Sure. Who do you think I'm going to tell?"

"All right. Now, I need to take you to the fight club, but since you didn't like Ben, I might take you elsewhere. It's a shame because the North Side club is one of the better ones. Tomkin manages it, not Ben. He isn't the best in higher rank training, but he's excellent for beginners."

"Do you want me to give that club another try?"

"Ben is no longer with that club, so I think you should give it another go. If you still don't like it, we can change later."

Sam nodded.

"I'll take you there," Alyna said and realized she wasn't dressed in her usual gear. Her hair was down, and she was wearing loose pants and a shirt without pockets for weapons. She shrugged. She shouldn't have to dress a certain way to prove she was a fighter who could kick ass. She signaled for Sam to follow her, and they headed toward the express subway.

Shortly, they approached the fight club. They were a block away, but she sensed something unusual happening. Trainees were walking out of the club, looking confused. Visitors looking for tickets for tonight's performance fight were being turned away.

She rushed into the club and saw Pukak talking to Tomkin. Tomkin's face paled when he saw her, and he stopped talking. Pukak looked at her, disappointed.

"What's up, Pukak?"

"Ben escaped."

"How? When?"

He sighed. "It appears he got away last night. Our surveillance didn't pick up anything. But Ben knew his way around here. He knew how not to be seen by the system." He chuckled. "If we have a functional system, that is."

"What does this have to do with me?" she asked.

"Why would you think Ben's escape has anything to do with you?" Tomkin asked.

Tomkin was a quiet guy. He rarely gave his opinion and always did what Pukak wanted. He wasn't a mage and thus couldn't progress in rank unless he entered fighting competitions—which he never did. So he just managed club business and trained beginners.

"I've always said I trusted Ben," Alyna said. "He has a temper, but he's not a traitor. True, the evidence was against him yesterday, but I feel we haven't given him enough opportunity to explain. That's just my view."

"Well, he's confirmed your belief, trust, and confidence in him, Alyna," Pukak said.

"What do you mean?"

Pukak handed her a note. She recognized Ben's handwriting. It was rare for people write anything by hand anymore, but Ben still did. The note stated, "I'm sorry to leave you like this, Alyna. I don't care what anyone else thinks. I only need you to believe I'll do what I promised you. I will never betray you, Alyna. Watch your back."

"I—"

Pukak cut in before she could utter another word. "You don't have to explain. He's your trainee and your confidant. Whatever you told him, we don't need to know."

When Pukak used the pronoun *we* with that tone of voice, it usually meant he had talked to outsiders who shouldn't be trusted.

"I had nothing to do with Ben's escape, Pukak. In fact, you might recall that I'm the one who captured him."

Pukak nodded. "What happened has happened. But it is our code that you cannot be included in our summoning ceremony."

"I couldn't care less, Pukak. I've told you before—I am not a mage, and I have no intention of being turned into one. I also have no intention of taking the spiritual leadership position."

"That's precisely the point. I understand now."

"Understand what?"

"You want to change Amaraq into a human-operated organization and abandon spiritual tradition."

"That's totally unfair, Pukak. How many years have I worked under you to build Amaraq and maintain the mage tradition? Has there been a single occasion when I deviated from that mission? Have I ever let you down?"

"You never failed a mission. But that's the problem. You recruited your trainees—Ben, the youngsters standing behind you now, and several who walked out of the club when I announced that you would no longer be in charge of their training."

"You announced what? *Why?*"

"You've turned Amaraq into something of your own. More than half the club left. Ben left. Can't you see the pattern, Alyna? They idolize you."

"I can't accept that accusation, Pukak. I should walk out of here right now, but I'm not going to do that. If you doubt my loyalty, if you think I have ill intentions, then use your light and purify me. I'll stand here and take it."

"What a challenge, Alyna! You know I would never hurt you."

"But you just did! What can I do to prove my loyalty?"

"I never doubted your loyalty. You've just outgrown Amaraq, that's all. We don't have enough to keep you here. Latch on to the LeBlancs—I'm sure they'll be able to arrange a very bright future for you in Mid-land London. The North just isn't for you, Alyna. Not anymore."

She turned and walked out of the club. She didn't know she was crying until Sam quietly handed her a piece of paper towel he had picked up from a food vendor on the street.

"Well, I don't have a job for you anymore, Sam. You can go now."

"I'm happy to tag along wherever you want to go."

"I need to be by myself."

Sam nodded. "All right, I'll look for you later then."

"Be good, Sam. Don't do anything you'll regret."

He grinned. "Amaraq doesn't deserve you, Alyna. Go South."

CHAPTER 19

Caedmon sauntered into the LeBlanc's headquarters as if he was oblivious to the fact that someone from within had been poking around for his information and had sent half a dozen high-end mercenaries after him. His records in the LeBlanc database were fake because he had come from the past, and so he had to be careful. He had no idea his records could be traceable.

Leanne rushed out from behind her desk. "Caedmon, you need more rest. Your bruises are still visible. Have you been to the medical center?"

"No, but I'll—"

"Don't underestimate your injuries. Maybe they're just flesh wounds, but until you get them properly scanned, I won't feel good about this."

"All right, I'll do it this afternoon. Do you know where Mr. Tann is by any chance?"

"Speak of the devil…" she said as Mr. Tann's voice drifted in from a side corridor.

"We just finished an executive meeting," he said and looked at Caedmon. "What happened to you?"

"A minor accident. I'm going to my office. I need the mainframe to connect to central. The system alerted me last night that someone tried to access classified data."

"Is that right? You mean from here?" asked Mr. Tann. "I didn't think our computers had the capacity to detect information regarding identity. That's only possible from Mid-land London."

Caedmon smiled. "I didn't say they'd tried to steal identity information."

"I just assumed." Tann smiled a crooked smile. "Identity is the most valuable kind of information. If someone had the guts to hack the LeBlanc's system, I'd automatically believe it had something to do with identity data."

Caedmon nodded. "Fair enough. And you're correct. It was identity information they were trying to steal."

"What a relief. I'm not an idiot after all."

Caedmon chuckled. "I don't think the LeBlancs have ever appointed idiots."

Tann shrugged. "They'd better not. Is there anything else I can do for you?"

Caedmon nodded. "Yes, I have something to show you." Then he turned toward Leanne. "I could do with some food. Given your warning about the north side of the city, I didn't eat anything when I was there."

"Right away. I'll get you something safe to eat," she said and scurried away.

Caedmon gestured for Tann to follow him into his office. Caedmon settled into his chair and turned on his computer. "When I finish my work here, Leanne will be transferred, working in Mid-land London. Do you know if she has any family or dependents here?"

Tann sat down opposite Caedmon. "If you want to take her with you, just take her. You don't have to pretend to care about her life."

"We might have differences, Mr. Tann, and I don't care to elaborate on them. But I—and any LeBlanc—value good employees and will do whatever it takes to make them happy. I must stress that this is how we treat top employees only."

"Okay. Leanne is a contractor here. We don't have any commitments with her. If you want to take her, then do so. She's not worth a discussion."

"So what *is* worth talking about, Mr. Tann? My secret identity?"

"Caedmon, if you want to accuse me of something, go for it. You don't look like the kind of guy to kill without reason."

Caedmon chuckled. "It's not a secret that you and I don't like each other. As I said, I don't intend to here for long. It really wasn't necessary to send mercenaries to scare me off. Just in case you haven't heard, they're all dead."

Mr. Tann shifted in his chair. The gesture, although subtle, showed signs of anxiety. *So you didn't know*, Caedmon thought and then said, "One of them provided me some information before he died," he said.

Mr. Tann stood up abruptly. "I don't know anything about this!"

"Are you saying you didn't send the mercenaries, or you didn't think one of them would have a chance to speak before he died. As you've already said, I'm not the kind who kills without reason."

"This is my turf, kid. Don't you dare threaten me."

"So you don't have an explanation about the mercenaries?"

"I don't have to explain anything to you. I don't report to you, and I don't answer to you." Mr. Tann strode toward the door.

Leanne came in, carrying a tray of food. Mr. Tann turned abruptly and followed behind her. He looked at Caedmon and then glanced at Leanne's backside.

Mr. Tann locked eyes with Caedmon and smirked. "Caedmon, how about I promise not to interfere in your business here, whatever it is. My staff and I won't interfere with you and Amaraq and whatever it is they're doing. In exchange, you will keep your nose out of my business here."

Caedmon said nothing, waiting for Leanne to arrange the food and exit the room.

"Your business is the LeBlanc business," said Caedmon. "If you act against our interests, I'll be forced to interfere with your operation. And I consider sending men after me, one of the LeBlancs, to be your shady operation."

"I had nothing to do with that!" he roared. He put both of his hands against the wall and shoved hard, sending a decorative picture crashing to the floor.

"There's no need to damage property. You're aware of the mercenaries."

"That doesn't mean I sent them."

Caedmon leaned back in his chair. "So who did then? One of them told me he was sent by someone in authority here."

"Well, we do have a board!"

"But you're the chairman."

"Are you from another planet?"

Caedmon rolled his eyes.

"Wait, you're from Mid-land London." Tann sneered. "That's like outer space to me. People here might work for you, but you don't own them. Loyalty and morality and all that shit existed only in ancient times, before the Great War. And if you ever bothered to study ancient history in the middle of the third millennium, you'd know it was that very idea of morality that sent humans to war."

"Religious war?"

Mr. Tann laughed. "Boy, you really know nothing. Religion is like patriotism. It encompasses loyalty and similar ideas. Humans made up those ideas and used them as guidelines for what they should do and what they should think. The Great War wiped out all of that. It took us back to bare bones. Good versus evil—or whatever you want to call it. Yes, the people on the board work for your money at the office. But outside of work, they might kill you to get the parking spot they want—and they won't see anything wrong with doing it."

"But the Amaraq people still operate on the principles of loyalty and morality."

"Caedmon, they aren't human!"

Caedmon shrugged. "Fair enough. So what you're saying is that someone on the board wants my head. You know about their activities, but you're not a part of them."

"And I won't acknowledge this conversation beyond these four walls. I dislike you enough to send you to the North side to get some bruises. But it's in my best interest that you stay alive because the LeBlanc business is my income." He nodded a goodbye and exited the room.

Leanne stuck her head in and smiled. "How's the deluxe sushi?" she asked.

CHAPTER 20

The Thunder Child looked at the Teacher, who was examining the basket of wildflowers and exotic mushrooms she had just collected for him in the woods. "What's your real name, Teacher?"

"You're suddenly not wanting to call me Teacher anymore?"

"I just want to know more about you and about your family and your children who were killed. It seems to me a good way to start a conversation like that is with your real name." She grinned at him.

"You're very mature for your age. I guess that's because of what happened to your parents. Have you ever wanted to talk about that?"

She shook her head.

"Then I won't tell you my story. It's only fair."

"Keymaster asked the same. He wants to know if I know who killed my parents."

"Do you?"

"I told him I saw some spider wolf creatures."

"Yes, but do you know who sent them? Your parents were angels. But that doesn't make you an angel, not until you dignify their death."

"I don't want to be an angel."

"What do you want to be then?"

She locked eyes with him. "What do you think your children would want to be if they hadn't been murdered?"

He sat down on a stone and gazed into the distance.

"I'm sorry if I made you sad," she said.

"It has been a hundred years. I'm no longer sad, Thunder Child."

"Does that mean you feel something different?" she asked. "Hatred? Anger? The need for vengeance?"

He brushed a stray hair from her forehead. "You think too much, child."

"The only time I didn't think was before the first blade pierced my father's body. Because I was an infant, I wasn't supposed to think. I hadn't even started talking. Then they stabbed my mother. They stabbed her again and again while she tried to crawl away from me so they wouldn't see me." Tears started to stream down her face.

"Come here, child!" He pulled her into his arms and held her.

"When Keymaster found me, I had to find a way to win him over. I had to make him like me so he would take me with him. I clapped my hands. I giggled. I cooed. I made baby noises. Because I was an infant, I couldn't speak, but I could still think, and I knew what had just happened to my parents." She started crying, and she knew the Teacher cried for her, too.

She had lost people she loved. So had he. They had to work together to seek revenge. She didn't know exactly what he wanted. But she knew what her life mission would be. She wanted justice for her parents. She knew who had sent the spiders. And she knew how to kill them.

But first, she needed to grow into the body of an adult. She needed to develop the necessary skills. She needed both Keymaster and the Teacher to support her and train her to become what she needed to be to get her revenge.

"If you had a choice, what would you want to be, Thunder Child?"

She smiled at the Teacher. "I don't know yet. I'm just a child."

CHAPTER 21

Alyna jabbed her finger at Caedmon's chest as soon as he turned the corner outside the LeBlanc's headquarters. "You killed Ben, didn't you?"

"How about some thanks for giving you the information that he's a rat? And if I remember correctly, he beat the hell out of me."

"I saw what you did to the guards at your complex. You're not human, Caedmon. And I think you could kill Ben if you wanted to."

He nodded. "What I am is irrelevant. I mean you and Amaraq no harm. I did have a conversation with Ben yesterday, and he asked me to tell you to be careful, especially with the summoning."

"You talked to him? Without us?"

"Well, the conversation was about you, and it wasn't about your taste in fashion. So you're right...our discussion didn't include you. I thought you could pull ranks within Amaraq to get Ben out if you liked him that much and believed he was innocent. He was alive and kicking when I left him."

"He escaped. I still don't believe he betrayed me, but there's nothing I can do with Amaraq now. They kicked me out."

Caedmon raised an eyebrow. "Their loss. At least you don't have to be involved in the summoning next week."

"It's not next week—it's next month. Next week is the trial. And I never planned to be involved. It's a huge event, so they have to practice. "

"Good. By the way, the head of the LeBlancs here just told me someone in-house wanted my head. Whoever it is sent six mercenaries, and we killed all of them. I'm going to need protection. Are you interested?"

She smiled. "You're more than capable of protecting yourself, Caedmon."

"I'm just a guy from out of town. Are you interested in the job or not?"

"Let me think about it."

"All right…"

"You forgot your sushi, Caedmon," Leanne said, stepping out from a corner of the room.

Alyna rolled her eyes and looked away.

"Leanne, you shouldn't have done this."

Leanne glanced at Alyna. "If you're going to the North side again, then please take the food. Eat it before you go."

She reached out to hand him the box with the sushi. As he touched it, a metal arrow pierced it just in front of his chest.

Alyna saw he had swiveled slightly to avoid the hit, and she applauded him for his instincts, but still she dove and pushed him over, falling to the ground with him.

"Get down!" she shouted to Leanne, who was still standing with the lunch box in her hands. She reached out and pulled Leanne to the ground. Leanne dropped the lunch box. Alyna pulled out the arrow and saw an E in fancy lettering on the shaft—the symbol of Ethesus.

"Bastards." She raced to the arrow's origin and chased the attacker into an alley where he stopped suddenly and turned toward her. He pulled down his hoodie and smirked.

It's a trap, she thought. She turned around to head back to Caedmon, but the man charged at her from behind. She could tell he was a high-ranking Ethesus. It would be a tough fight.

The man anticipated her every move, and she couldn't even get to her guns. After a few rounds, she managed to kick the man away and reach for her weapons. But then he threw a smoke bomb and darted around the corner.

It was a sedative bomb, and she had inhaled the powder. She dropped to her knees. Her world started to spin. He arms seemed to weigh a ton. With great effort, she pushed herself to her feet and struggled back toward Caedmon. When she was out of the alley, she saw him battling a group of five across the street.

She collapsed to her knees again. She had plenty of willpower, but her body wasn't cooperating. Hearing footsteps behind her, she glanced back and saw the man she had fought before. He approached, knife in hand.

From across the street, Caedmon could see her situation. She wanted to tell him not to worry, not to be distracted, but she didn't know how. She couldn't speak, and her world was dimming by the second. In her last moment of blurred vision, she saw that the distraction had cost Caedmon.

He pulled a dart from his neck. His knees buckled. The men he was fighting launched an increased attack to be sure he was incapacitated. And then he was down.

Leanne ran out from a side street with the same lunch box she had tried to hand Caedmon. She swung it at the men. One of them yanked it away from her, and she started slapping at them, swinging her purse and kicking at them with her stiletto heels. Alyna had to give it to her—she was brave. But the men stopped her feminine assault in no time.

All Alyna could do now was crawl toward them, making sure her movement didn't draw any attention.

Across the road, two men carried Caedmon to a car that had just arrived and parked next to the sidewalk. A third man knocked out Leanne with a single punch and threw her inside the car.

As the car drove away, Alyna felt the hand of the man behind her pulling her up by the hair. She could feel the metal blade of a knife pressed against her throat.

Then she was released. There was the sound of a fight and a struggle from behind her. She didn't even have the energy to turn her head to see what was happening. And then, someone turned her over. Ben was smiling down at her.

CHAPTER 22

Caedmon opened his eyes groggily. He felt unbearably tired. He may be supernatural, but he never did well with sedatives, no matter what universe he was in. He hadn't turned on his eudqi during the fight before he passed out, and he was glad he'd made that decision. He had no idea what the consequences would be if he had been sedated with his super power on.

He wondered what had happened to Alyna and Leanne. He sat up, trying to get his bearings.

Once upright, he realized his worst nightmare—his wrist unit was gone. It held all the top secrets of Eudaiz—his make, his DNA, and most importantly, what could kill a Eudaizian. No one could operate the unit but him, but if the reason for taking the unit had been to extract data, he was doomed.

He tugged at the metal handcuffs that held him captive. He had no chance of getting out as a human. At the moment, what others might see him as was no longer a concern. Getting the unit back was his top priority, so he not only turned on his eudqi, but also the Silver Blood, a super energy that not everyone in Eudaiz could access. In his mind, he gathered his most natural and significant talents to create a giant blade.

He used that blade to cut into the place where they held him captive. His mind blades sliced through the concrete and metal, and the grating sounds shook the building. He heard the footsteps of men rushing out to see what was happening. He turned on his internal microchip and scanned the building.

Leanne was in another room, two doors down from him. His wrist unit was on the upper level, in a room that appeared to be a computer room.

They wanted to extract the data.

Caedmon could feel his rage surging. He concentrated, trying to recreate the effects of his newfound skill that had killed two guards with a combination of heat and combustion.

He summoned his rage by focusing on his negative energy and emotions. He could feel the heat rising in his veins, but instead of causing an explosion as he had before, he directed the heatwave into a small blade, and with laser precision, he cut through the handcuffs.

The heat burned his flesh, so he took some time to heal himself. The wounds would be inconvenient in an upcoming fight. Then he went to the far end of the room. He stood there, staring at the metal door. He blasted an extreme heatwave to the door to soften the metal. Then he charged at it and gave it a hard kick. The softened hinges released, and the door collapsed.

Using his new talent seemed to drain his energy quickly. He needed more time to learn how to control it. But right now, it was available and he could use it to his advantage.

Three guards inside the building rushed at him. He waited until they got close, and when two of them grabbed him, he pumped heatwaves into them. Like the guards he had killed before, these two exploded. The third ran away. He picked up a gun from one of the dead guards and shot the third one. He didn't see any keys on the floor near the two guards, so he searched the body of the third and found a key.

Caedmon rushed to Leanne's cell and opened the door. She was cringing in a corner, but when she saw him, she ran into his arms.

"Are you okay?" he asked.

She nodded. "And you?"

"I'm fine, but they took something from me that I have to get back. There will be a fight, so I want you to stay behind me at all times. Understood?"

She nodded and scurried after him.

The hall was wider on the upper level, and quiet. It looked as if most the staff had gone out to see the destruction he had caused outside. He wondered what it might look like.

Caedmon found the computer room easily. A single engineer remained. Caedmon entered the room, gun pointed at the man, who raised his arms.

"Take whatever you want," he said. "I just work here. I don't care what you take. I won't make a sound."

Caedmon, gun pointed at the man, strode toward the far end of a long table where his wrist unit was connected to four computers. He grabbed the unit from the table and disconnected the wires. Then he pointed the gun at the engineer. "Delete the data. Now."

The engineer didn't wait for a second request. He ran to the keyboard and entered commands to delete all data.

From the door, Leanne said, "They're coming back."

The progress bar on the monitor indicated eighty percent completion of deletion. The footsteps came closer. Before Caedmon could stop her, Leanne exited to the hallway. She smiled at the approaching engineers.

"Hello!"

Caedmon was surprised to hear the friendly greeting. The engineers didn't seem to have a clue what was going on in the prison section.

As Leanne started a conversation with the engineers, the happy ping of deletion completion sounded on the computer.

"Don't make a sound until we're out of the building," he told the engineer in the room. "You don't want casualties. I don't, either. Understood?"

The engineer nodded. He turned on a computer game and began playing it as if nothing was going on.

Caedmon walked out casually and called to Leanne. "It's time to go, honey!"

She grinned. "That's my boyfriend. Sorry, I have to go." She walked to his side, leaving a very disappointed group of engineers behind.

Together, they walked down the corridor and out of the building. As soon as they stepped outside, someone yelled at them from behind.

"Hey!"

Caedmon didn't turn around. He knew what it meant. "Run," he said.

They ran along a wide street into an open area that looked like a market. No one so much as gave them a curious glance as they were chased through the market at gunpoint. Caedmon gave up hope that anyone would question violence in a public place. This was normal life on New Earth. It sucked.

Caedmon glanced back and saw that one of the people chasing them had raised a gun. He had to act first. He shot down the gunman.

If they could make it across the street, he could get Leanne to the back alley, and there, he would be able to kill the man chasing them. He glanced back again and saw four of them.

"Cross the street, Leanne."

She nodded at him and turned. As soon as she turned back to continue to run, he watched as a bullet—as if in slow motion—penetrated her body from the back and exploded out the front.

He turned and fired. He didn't care whether there were innocent bystanders. He just pulled the trigger. Again and again. Soon their pursuers were down. He rushed over to Leanne, who was lying in a pool of her own blood.

CHAPTER 23

Alyna bolted upright, gasping and panting. She saw Ben grinning at her, but before she could make a move, he said, "Remember, I risked my neck to save your pretty ass, Alyna. So you should think twice before you kick mine."

She jumped off the bed. "Where's Caedmon?" she asked and rushed toward the door.

"You're welcome," Ben said and headed toward the kitchen to make himself something to eat.

Alyna was back, standing at the door. "I meant to say thank you. I know you're always looking out for me, and I appreciate it. I'll do the same for you. I promise."

He nodded.

She nodded her goodbye and left the apartment.

***

Caedmon used his microchip to help navigate to a medical center. He carried Leanne in his arms. She was so quiet it scared him. She was no longer gasping for air. Blood seeped from her wound, soaking into his shirt and dripping to the ground as he walked.

Nobody around them cared.

He kept walking.

She stirred and opened her eyes.

"There you are. I'm going to find a medical center. You're going to be okay."

"Put me down, Caedmon."

"We're nearly there."

"Put me down, please."

He put her down on the sidewalk. She looked at him and smiled.

"I'm not going to make it, Caedmon. Everyone dies someday, and I guess my number is up."

"I won't accept that. If the medical center can't fix you, I will."

"No, Caedmon, just let it go. You hardly know me."

"If you survive this, I'll take you to Mid-land London. You can work for me there. I'll make sure you're taken care of."

"You're very kind. It was my honor to work for you, even if only for a short period of time. Go back to Mid-land London. This place isn't for you."

"Leanne, I'm not entirely human. I have a special sort of energy that could help heal you. Will you agree to take my energy?"

"Why, Caedmon? Death isn't bad at all. I'll be free of this world. I'm not sad to be leaving it."

"Please accept my energy. You can make the decision where to live later."

She smiled weakly. "I am ready to leave this world behind, Caedmon."

"Please don't say that. Let me do this for you. Please."

"You're crying." She reached her hand up to touch his face. "No one's ever cried for me before. I would never have thought someone would cry when I die. Just that small gesture is worth dying for... Do you know how beautiful you are? Do you know how strong a man is when he allows himself to cry? I'm grateful for that… Remember, Caedmon… I am dying a very happy woman… I'm so cold… Would you hold me?"

He pulled her into his arms and held her. In a few moments, she stopped breathing.

A man approached Caedmon. "Private or public waste, sir?"

"What?"

"If she's private waste, please take her inside. Or I can take her now if not. My truck is just over there." He pointed at a truck that was picking up trash cans along the street.

"Don't you dare call her waste!" he shouted. There must have been something in his eyes that scared the man. In only two steps, the man had scooted across the street, cursing as he rushed away.

Caedmon picked up Leanne's body and started walking along the street. He had no idea where he was going.

***

Alyna turned around the corner and saw Caedmon standing in the middle of the street, holding Leanne's body in his arms and looking totally confused and upset. She had used all her resources to trace him. And here he was, free from the hub of Ethesus. Leanne was an unfortunate casualty. But there was nothing she could do to change that.

She approached him. "Let them take her body, Caedmon."

"They called her waste," he growled.

She had never seen such grief from a man for a stranger. She didn't know what kind of creature he was, but she certainly hadn't seen anything like this from humans. "It's just terminology, Caedmon. What would you like to do with the body?"

"I'd like to help her family arrange a proper burial."

"No one here has access to free land for burials. Maybe where you come from, but not here. Free land is so limited that it's not allowed to be used for burying anything or anyone. The men who handle this process know best what to do with the body. It's their business. She will be treated best by them."

He looked back at the waste truck suspiciously.

"Or you can leave her out here to rot…"

He nodded. She walked toward the truck, and the driver took a step back in defense. She raised her hands so he could see she had no weapons and meant him no harm. She then pulled out a few credit tokens.

"I'm so sorry. My friend is really upset about her death. They were close. If he scared you, I apologize. Here, please take this money and take care of the body.

It's going to be public w—" She stopped herself. "It will be a public matter."

The man looked her up and down and then reluctantly accepted the money. He called out to another man, and they approached Caedmon with a stretcher.

As they wheeled the stretcher back to their truck, they passed Alyna. She overheard one of the men say, "This is the last one for today. I'm not taking any more random jobs."

"It's only early afternoon."

"Well, picking up twelve at the Amaraq fight club was tough. I'd call it a month's worth of work."

She rushed over. "Excuse me, which club are you talking about?"

"North Side."

"Who are the casualties?"

"I think it's the guards," one of the men said.

The other shook his head. "It can't be. They're the best fighters. Plus they looked pretty young. I think they must have been trainees."

"Do you know the cause of death?"

"Accident. A fighting room's roof collapsed."

She pulled out her communication unit and called Pukak. There was no answer. The line was totally dead.

CHAPTER 24

Pukak looked at what remained of the North Side fight club. He sighed. The building would be out of action for a long time and certainly couldn't be used to host the trial for the summoning next week. They had no other facility that could do the job. He might end up having to use their temple. Not only was that not ideal, but it was also dangerous, especially now that he had lost Alyna and Ben.

He glanced at the manager of the club, Tomkin, and watched as he fished around in the rubble, pulled up bits and pieces of shrapnel, and stumbled over things. He wasn't sure Tomkin could actually fight these days. As a human, he was quite old for his job. Pukak made a mental note to revamp the entire training program and put mage staff in place for anything related to martial arts. Humans were good, but their life span was limited, and their skills and strength depreciated exponentially with age.

Tomkin rushed over. "I've cleaned up the stadium and the fighting platform, Pukak. We can use it now. What do you think?" He gestured and grinned.

Pukak turned and saw a patched-up area. Temporary panels and sheets of plastic had been used to patch holes in the walls. Sticks of wood were nailed to the platforms where the audience sat to bolster the legs of the benches that accommodated twenty people each. But Pukak was sure if he set foot on the platform as it was now, it would collapse.

"Tomkin, how many people do you think this venue can hold, and how many do you think will come to the event?"

"You mean the trial?"

"Yes, the trial."

"A handful." He looked at the expression on Pukak's face. "Twenty? No?"

"We will host one hundred and two senior members from all the clubs across Old and New Sydney,

Central Americana, Underground Asiana, and the African Transition. Even if we can fit them in here, do you think what you have done there will represent us in a good light in front of our allies?"

Tomkin shook his head. "How about we book a venue in the city? Just for show, you know."

"And of course, you would pay for that?"

Tomkin shook his head. "I told you this is Ethesus's doing. We don't have haters. I mean we do, but they wouldn't throw explosives at us right when we need the venue most. They wouldn't kill our trainees. They're in competition with us, and they've fought for years for the right to host the summoning."

"Well, that's a very smart and thoughtful comment, Tomkin. But even if it's true, and if—and this is a very big if–we could find evidence that Ethesus stabbed us in the back, that's not the solution to our problem right now."

"Yes, it is. We can demand compensation. We can find evidence and make them pay. And then we can use that money to get new accommodations."

"All in a week? And who do you think would enforce the compensation demand? I'm too old for a fight." He thought of Alyna again and sighed.

Then there was a loud bang. The building shook, and idirt gushed out as the pressure of an explosion was forced out from the back of the building. Pukak and Tomkin were thrown nto the front wall like rag dolls.

I must have passed out for a second, Pukak thought as he scrambled to his feet and rushed over to Tomkin, who was sitting up on the floor, coughing and heaving from the dust.

"Are you okay? Can you get up by yourself?" Pukak asked.

Tomkin nodded and grabbed a piece of the remaining wall at waist height to help him stand. The wall collapsed under his weight into a pile of loose bricks.

Pukak shook his head as he looked around. More casualties. As he turned, a dozen premier Ethesus fighters stepped out from the smoke and dirt. He recognized their leather outfits and the symbols on their arm shields and masks.

They approached him, slowly and stealthily. When he was younger, he would have been excited about the opportunity to fight them. But not now. Not in this situation. They weren't here to have a fight with the glorious leader of one of the oldest mage tribes in history. They had been sent here to finish him after the explosion.

Pukak flexed his muscles. He would fight until his last breath. And that would come soon.

Tomkin rushed over to stand by him. "Hey! All of you against two of us, and after planting a bomb? You should be ashamed of yourselves."

The fighters said nothing. They charged at the two Amaraq men. But only three of them came at a time. Pukak knew it wasn't because they were trying to play fair. It was just that there wasn't enough room for them all to come at once.

He wanted to tell Tomkin to stay inside to retain their advantage. But he didn't have time to talk and didn't think Tomkin was smart enough to understand.

After the first round, both sides withdrew. They had drawn some blood from the Ethesus fighters. Pukak was pleased by that. He glanced across and saw that Tomkin had suffered some minor injuries but was still standing. Ethesus fighters prepared to charge for a second round. Pukak knew he couldn't sustain this level of fighting for long.

This round, they squeezed in eight fighters. Withdrawing wasn't an option because then they would attack them from behind. Pukak pressed on and stepped forward.

As the fighters came closer, Pukak felt a rush of fresh air coming from behind. He didn't need to look—he felt instant relief. Alyna landed in front of him, coming down from the rooftop.

"Welcome to Amaraq North Side fight club," she said and charged at them. They probably wouldn't be able to see much as she moved like a leopard.

"There have been enough casualties for one day," said Alyna. "I'll take four of you as payback for our trainees, and I'll let the rest live to crawl back to your boss and let him know your humiliation."

An Ethesus fighter at the far left pulled out a small device, but before he could do anything with it, Alyna put a bullet in his head. "One."

A fighter on the right went for his gun, but Alyna fired before the gun left his holster. "Two. Any more volunteers?"

"Get down!" she shouted at Pukak and Tomkin, anticipating that the remaining Ethesus would draw their guns. Alayna moved to the side. The bullets missed her and hit the walls. At the same time, Pukak heard other gunshots, and the Ethesus fighters fell one by one like tree trunks.

From behind them, Ben and Caedmon walked out, guns in hand.

Alyna helped Pukak up from the ground. "Three of us against twelve of them. We were still outnumbered, Pukak, so don't whine that they didn't have a fair fight because we hit them in their backs."

"Since when do I whine?"

CHAPTER 25

Caedmon strode into LeBlanc headquarters, making a beeline for his office. This time, Leanne wouldn't be giving him her usual greeting, checking on what he was going to eat and where he needed to go, or telling him about the places and things he should avoid. She had taken good care of him, and because she did such a good job, she had gotten herself killed.

He turned on the computer, and it flashed a message asking for verification. He frowned. It hadn't asked for that before. The credentials he'd created for this trip were impeccable. He a LeBlanc, and in that regard, he hadn't needed to fake any data.

He typed in his credentials.

A dialog box popped up. "Access denied."

He re-entered the information

The computer repeated, "Access denied."

The door slid open. Mr. Tann stood in the doorway, hands in pockets.

"People in Old Australia don't knock?" Caedmon asked.

"I would knock if it was your office I was entering." He walked in.

Caedmon sank back into his chair, watching as Mr. Tann sauntered in and sat in a chair in front of his desk.

"What can I do for you, Caedmon?"

"We purchased Amaraq, and I'd like to transfer funds to them."

"I've checked with central London. They confirmed that no such purchase plan exists."

"I don't believe you have access to our records. But I have to hand it to you, for a moment I thought you might have a spy in the London office. But that's not possible because you don't have connections of that caliber. The only plausible explanation is that some members of your shady board have connections. And they poked their nose into my business."

"You poked yours into our business first. Yes, my board members have checked the records, and Caedmon LeBlanc doesn't exist at this point in time. Your DNA is confirmed, but your existence is not."

"Well, that depends on how far backward—or forward—the system can trace."

Mr. Tann stood up. "You're a vampire?"

"I can walk in sunlight, so I can't be a vampire." Caedmon chuckled. "But why would you assume I come from the past?"

"We're heading toward the millennium. There's nothing the system can see in the future."

"Are you talking about the end of the world? I think I've heard about that a few times."

"No, I'm talking about changes. There are going to be radical changes, and I don't know which way it will go. Like the Great War. Nobody saw it coming. When it happened, it wiped out the entire societal structure of human civilization. And technology went with it. Thus, I see no point in looking forward."

Caedmon leaned forward. "Between you and me, my records existed long before the Great War."

"Are you saying your records were conveniently destroyed?"

Caedmon leaned back in his chair and locked eyes with Mr. Tann. "Do you think knowing too much could potentially cause you harm?"

"Is that a threat?"

"Why would I bother making a threat? I'm a LeBlanc. You said so yourself. But yes, there are things I do that I wouldn't care for my extended family to know about. It's my business," he said. "I'll stick to the promise I made to you when we first met. Amaraq is my only business here. When I'm finished, I'll be out of here in a heartbeat. The sooner you let me get on with my business, the quicker you'll be rid of me."

"I'll check with my board and get back to you." Mr. Tann said and stood to leave the office.

Caedmon surged up from his chair, jumped over the desk, and grabbed Mr. Tann by the neck. He pulled him back into the room and slammed his face on the desk. "By sooner, I mean *now!* There are many ways to do this. Why would you choose the hard way?"

"You don't know who you're dealing with, Caedmon. The LeBlancs may have money, but you are very much out of touch here. As I said, you don't own people's morality."

Caedmon slammed his head on the desk again. "Exactly! So you don't have to hold your moral standards to your faceless board!"

"Regarding the board, I'm not talking about morality. I only want to survive. And trust me, they are not faceless."

"Then show me their faces."

Silence.

Caedmon was about to slam his head again.

"All right, all right! I take it you're a man of your word. I'll help you get on with your business—but please leave after that. I don't care about Amaraq or whatever it is they're doing."

Caedmon released him. "All right, I need the funds. Right now."

"I'm sorry, Caedmon. I can help with your locked computer. I can issue a special pass. But that's about it. I can't let you transfer funds the board is aware of. And I can't tell you who they are. I don't want to end up like Leanne."

Caedmon grabbed him by the collar. "You knew they sent people after me and got Leanne killed? What's their connection with Ethesus?"

"I'm a dead man walking, Caedmon!" He pushed him away. "I'll get you a passcode for the computer. Then—"

Blood splattered all over Caedmon. He looked up to see that Mr. Tann's face exploded. He had been hit from behind.

Caedmon dropped to the floor and pulled his gun. He switched his eudqi on and heard the stealthy footsteps of mercenaries. He turned on his microchip to scan the exterior of the office. A small army of more than twenty fighters was rushing into a corridor, heading toward him. The bodies of the office staff littered the floor.

He glanced up at the open window. Judging from the angle of the shot to Mr. Tann's head, the kill shot had come from an assailant located outside the building. A hit man.

A gunfight between himself and twenty others with machine guns wouldn't be wise, and singlehandedly fighting this small army wasn't exactly the ideal combat situation, either. He didn't want to garner the attention of the wrong people, but this was the perfect time to make good use of his talent.

He concentrated, trying to use his most lethal skill set—he willed a mind blade, and he sliced the building in two from the outside. The blade separated the building into halves, stopping the mercenaries short before they could get to his temporary office.

The gap between the two halves of the building was widening quickly, however. The building would soon separate and then collapse. He couldn't remember which floor he was on... He could feel his half of the building shaking.

He opened the office window and looked down. He was ten stories from the ground. He had many talents—the mind blade was his strongest and most important, and the heatwave was a new one for him.

But there was one talent he knew he would never have…flying.

.

CHAPTER 26

Alyna came back to the center of what used to be the fighting platform of Amaraq's North Side fight club. Around her were loose bricks, broken furniture, and bits and pieces of walls and the roof. Tomkin grabbed a shovel and started digging, making an attempt to clean things up and hoping there was still a chance he could repair the building with his bare hands in time to use it for the summoning trial next week.

Alyna understood that the club was his baby. He had worked here his whole life. The summoning was a centennial event, and being able to host just the trial for it had been his lifetime dream. But she saw no chance of the event happening here.

"Tomkin!"

"What?" he asked and kept digging.

"Tomkin!"

"I'm busy here! What do you want, Alyna?"

"The building is ruined, and so many trainees have lost their lives. The trial is not going to happen here next week. I suggest you focus your energy on something else."

He stabbed the shovel hard into a pile of dirt and loose bricks. "Like what?"

"Develop new programs. Talk to the families of the dead trainees. Do damage control for our reputation with the public. No one is going to use our private security service if we can't protect our own people. You're good at publicity. Why don't you take care of that, and I'll take care of the trial."

"I want to be at the trial. I'm not a mage, so I won't be invited to the summoning. But can I please be at the trial? It's a centennial event!"

Alyna nodded. "I'll talk to Pukak."

"Why don't you ask Ben to stay and help?" he asked as she turned around to leave.

"I respect his decision to go South. He'll do better there, I think."

She looked at the clock and wondered where Caedmon was. He'd said he was going to drop by the LeBlanc headquarters in central to transfer the money so that Amaraq could use it to hire a new venue in town for the event. It seemed like the perfect solution to her.

She headed toward the express to go home. She lived in the middle of the city, and hopefully it was close enough to central so that she could give Caedmon assistance in case he needed her. She chuckled inwardly. Since when had she started to think that a man would mix with someone like her in such a social circus?

She recalled the moment he carried her out of Tony's place. The feeling of her body pressed against his. The sensual scent emanating from his skin. His hands on her body, unclasping her bra, loosening her hair.

She shook her head and gave herself a mental slap.

By the time she approached the corner of her place, dusk had settled on the city. The sky was magnificent. She loved the blood red sky scattered with mysterious black clouds. She wondered what it had been like before the Great War. Pukak immersed himself in literature and loved history. He knew a lot. She wasn't a fan of curating knowledge of a culture that no longer existed. She was pro-development and all about moving forward.

"Alyna!" Sam called from behind.

She turned around and saw him standing in the alleyway running along the side of her complex. He had the gray cat in his arms—the one she'd claimed was hers—and he was grinning at her.

She approached him. "Where did you find him?"

"I didn't. He found me."

The cat hopped out of Sam's arms, landed on the ground, and sauntered toward Alyna.

"He could have found you himself, I think. But he's quite lazy. Look at the weight on him. He just wanted me to carry him all the way here." Sam laughed as the cat rubbed around Alyna's legs.

"His name is Lazi, Sam."

"Oh…well, that explains it."

From the corner of her eyes, she saw a creature step out from the darkness into the red light of the dusk. It didn't have a tangible form but appeared instead to be a collection of semitransparent black particles. It was the same thing that had jumped out of Tony's dead body and strangled her.

Alyna staggered back, and the cat scurried to find a hiding place.

"What is it, Alyna?" Sam asked.

"Run, Sam. Go away."

"No! Just tell me what's going on."

"There's something here. It's going to attack me. You can't see it…"

It flew at her. As much as it was invisible to Sam, it felt like a ton of bricks hitting her. It started squeezing her neck, just as it had done before, but she couldn't defend herself. She swung her arms at it, but they struck thin air. The creature continued to strangle her.

Sam darted over, but he didn't know what to do.

The cat jumped toward Alyna, hitting the creature with its front legs. It was small in comparison to the size of the creature, but the creature staggered back and hissed at the feline.

Alyna gasped for air and then scrambled to her feet. The cat stood in front of her, meowing and hissing. Its hair stood on end, its eyes sparkled green, and its teeth were bared. The creature stood immobile, a lump of static particles. It dared not move against Lazi—her dead cat.

"Sam, come stand behind me!" she shouted.

But it was too late for Sam. The creature flew over her head. Sam didn't see it coming. It lifted him up and dragged him away, several feet above the ground. It choked him, and then it slaughtered him.

"Lazi, get it! Over there!" she shouted, but the cat wouldn't leave her side. She charged toward Sam. But she knew she was too late.

The skinny body of the teenager was mangled, and his neck was broken. His soft green eyes stared into nothingness. He never knew what had hit him.

But she knew.

It was evil. She didn't know how to describe it.

Tears streamed down her face. She hadn't cried in a long time. And now she was crying for a person she hardly knew.

She looked up and saw the sky was completely dark. She understood now how Caedmon had felt when people had called Leanne's dead body waste. She couldn't bear the thought of Sam lying in the dark alley, waiting for the trash truck to come to pick him up in the morning. But she couldn't just take him inside the building. The other residents would object to it.

She went into her apartment and grabbed a blanket. She wrapped up Sam's body and propped him up against the fence next to the trash cans. Then she sat down next to his body. She would wait there until the morning to be sure he was taken care of and treated properly.

Lazi sat down next to her and purred for a while. Then the cat stood and started meowing. He bit her finger gently, and then bit into the sleeve of her shirt and pulled.

"I won't go with you, Lazi. I made that decision years ago. And I'm not changing my mind. You can go, though."

The cat didn't look happy, but he sat down next to her and stopped protesting. She stroked his head. "When the time comes, I'll respond to the Teacher's call. But not now."

As if he understood what she was saying, Lazi started purring again, tilting his head up for Alyna to scratch his neck.

CHAPTER 27

Caedmon was on the way down. It was a risky decision, but it was his best choice. He had just cut the giant high rise in half with his mind blade, and both sides were on the verge of collapse—and he was on the ledge of the tenth floor.

His eudqi was on at full capacity, and now he moved as a Silver Blood—lightning fast and agile, and he could jump dimensions. Admittedly, his dimension-jumping technique had room for improvement. He couldn't just jump by himself—he had to rely on the technology of his wrist unit to open the gateway before he did so. He opened the portal below him so he could use gravity to his advantage and fall right into the gateway.

From the corner of his eye, he saw the shape of the dematerialized creature—the same kind of thing that had tried to kill Alyna and had attacked him in the apartment. He had killed one of them with his heatwave, and he could do it again. But this one was incredibly fast. It flew into the air and hit him when he least expected it.

It knocked him out of his trajectory to the gateway. He was now free falling.

He adjusted his wrist unit to alter the gateway's position. But the creature struck him again. He was halfway down to the ground. The gravity on Earth was stronger than he'd expected.

The creature approached him again. It didn't give him a chance to manage the escape hatch. He turned around.

"You asked for it," he said.

He stopped fidgeting with the gateway. When the creature hit him again, he grabbed it and hopped on top of it, not sure whether he'd be able to grab its semitransparent form. But apparently, he could.

It wriggled, turned around, and was upside down. It looked at him. Its form glowed in a shimmery red color, and he could see its face more clearly—hollow red eyes and a face that looked like nothing more than a human skull. It reached its arms up, trying to strangle him.

He'd had enough. He pumped a heatwave into it. It exploded into several thousand pieces, accompanied by the sound of shattering glass. He was sure it had dropped pieces of red ice to the ground as had the one he'd killed before. But he had no intention of finding out. If he did, it would mean he had hit the ground.

He was close now. And he wasn't sure he had enough space for another portal. He looked up. The one he had opened previously still hovered in the air above him. The gateway refused to come down to him.

He looked down to the ground. He didn't relish the idea of his body landing on the hard concrete.

Another shadow zoomed toward him. Before he could blast out another heatwave, he realized it was giant air motorbike. The driver dipped down a bit, partially to indicate to Caedmon he had no intention of hitting him, and partially to make it easy for him to jump on the backseat.

No matter who the driver might be, Caedmon figured the backseat of an air motorbike was a much more promising option than the hard concrete fifty feet below.

Caedmon jumped on the bike.

***

A short moment later, the motorbike landed in an industrial area. The ground was covered in red dust, and they appeared to be on the outskirts of the city. From where they were, Caedmon could see the city covered by a semitransparent dome. He guessed they had passed through the dome's gate at some point, but he hadn't felt the impact.

He had turned his eudqi off to avoid a scan and detection from whomever he might be talking to. They'd known he wasn't human when they sent the driver to pick him up in the middle of the fight with a supernatural creature. But he didn't want them to know exactly where he had come from. He wasn't going to give them entry into Eudaiz.

The driver hopped off the bike and gestured for Caedmon to follow him. A wall-sized rusty steel door slid open, revealing a warehouse-style space. Everything was made of oxidized metal and wood of some sort. Several air motorbikes were scattered around as used for furniture.

At the far end of the open space, there was a raised platform of metal bars and wooden panels. A man sitting on a metal chair stood and approached Caedmon. He reached out a bare, muscled arm, covered in tattoos, for a handshake.

"Nathan," he said.

"Caedmon."

Nathan grinned. "One of the LeBlancs." He gestured around. "This is the deep North of New Australia, but your family has a reputation everywhere."

Caedmon nodded. "Thanks for picking me up at the headquarters. So I guess you're not the one who sent the mercenaries after me?"

Nathan laughed. "Did any of them look like my guys?"

Caedmon cast a glance at the bikers. "No. But nothing would stop you from having someone else do the work for you."

Nathan laughed again, climbed the platform, and sat on his chair. Caedmon realized the chair looked like a lot like a throne.

"You're Ethesus!"

Nathan clapped. "Unlike what people have said, the LeBlancs do know something the North."

"I guess you haven't invited me here for a party, then?"

"Not at all. Wartime is coming. No time for partying."

"War with whom? Amaraq?"

"Oh no, I don't consider them enemies. I know they don't see the dynamics of our relationship the same way."

"You captured me and killed Leanne. It's hard for me to consider you a friend."

"Not friend, but an ally. Look at us." Nathan gestured around. "Yes, spiritually we are on the opposite side of Amaraq. I offered an alliance, but they turned it down. We don't use technology for anything other than watching screens. You were captured and brought to a place with a full lab and lots of computer geeks, right? They used sedatives, and they copied our logo, too? But take another look...do we look like them?"

"So who are they?"

Nathan smirked. "I'll find out. And I'll crush them to dust. But to do that, we'll need financial backing. I know you promised that to Amaraq. But we can work together...as an alliance. Pukak can't see the big picture. But you can—"

Caedmon raised his hand to stop his speech. "I don't have the money. At least not right now. You picked me up from the headquarters. That was only connection I had. Now I'm cut off, and I'm not sure how long it will take to reconnect, let alone transfer any funds."

"But when you reconnect, will you reconsider my proposal? We'll stay within our red dirt areas in the outskirts, and Amaraq will stay where they are in the central. No invasions, no harsh feelings. And I reckon whoever it is who's disguising themselves as us and causing friction between Amaraq and Ethesus is our common enemy. The funds should be used to destroy that enemy…not to fight each other like mad dogs."

"Any idea where this common enemy might come from?"

"The South."

CHAPTER 28

Thunder Child threw a knife at the dummy and hit it right in the center of its forehead. The Teacher clapped.

"In terms of fighting, I think you've graduated. You've achieved a lot in such a short period of time."

"It's been two years. That's not a short period of time."

"Don't be impatient. You're young. You have plenty of time."

"I'm eleven. That's not so young."

The Teacher chuckled. "Well, compared to being a few hundred years old, you're very young."

"Will you teach me new skills?"

"Yes, of course. How's your master doing with the Scorpio key? Still trying to cut the stone?"

She sighed and nodded.

"All right." The Teacher wrote on a piece of old fabric. "Here are the ingredients. This compound, if you process it correctly, will both soften the stone and help it maintain its shape after it's been cut. It won't return to its original shape."

She grinned and reached out her hand to take the recipe, but the Teacher yanked it away. "It's too soon for me to give this to you. This compound works, but it isn't harmless. If you want me to give it to you now, I'll need you to do something for me."

"What is it, Teacher?"

He showed her a jar of potion. "This is a poison I have compounded. I will take you into town, and you will put it into someone's food."

"You want me to kill?"

"Yes."

"Whose food?"

"I have found the murderers of my children. I could simply kill them, but that would be too easy for them, considering I have suffered for hundreds of years. So I'm going to take you to a school of magic where their children are studying. You will kill their children. I want them to feel what it's like to lose a young child."

"But your children died hundreds of years ago. How can their children still be going to school?"

"They're soul traders. They buy, sell, and exchange souls so that they and their families will remain the same age for eternity."

"I can't kill innocent children."

"Not even to get the recipe for your master?"

"No."

"What if I give you something more appealing? What if I give you a recipe that will help you kill those who killed your parents?"

She chuckled. "They can't be killed with poison."

"You know them?"

She locked eyes with the Teacher. "Yes, and one day I will kill them. But not with poison. I will kill them to seek justice for my parents, but I won't kill innocent people just to make them experience what I have suffered my whole life. I won't do that for you, either. Not for anyone."

"There is a prophecy that says if I seek revenge, I will be dead. Nevertheless, I can't pass up this opportunity. So if I don't see you next time in the woods, you'll know what happened."

"If you die, I will seek revenge for you."

He crouched and looked into her eyes. "Really?"

"Yes, I promise. Who are they?"

"Amaraq."

CHAPTER 29

Alyna rushed into the medical clinic, almost stumbling on the bucket Pukak used to catch rainwater to make his medicine. Caedmon trailed behind her.

"Please tell me this isn't true," she said.

Pukak looked at her, the kind old eyes of a grandfather drooping even more. He pulled up his sleeve, revealing a wound that ran down his left forearm. "I know my time is limited, Alyna."

"You're a mage. You make medicines that cure people." She wiped the tears from her face. "There's no poison that exists that doesn't have an antidote. Can't you make yourself one?"

"Alyna…I don't have much time. I need you to listen to me."

"This was Ethesus. This is their doing," she snarled and whirled back and forth in the little office.

Caedmon grabbed her, but she couldn't be held still. "You can't be sure this was an Ethesus job," he said. "I talked to Nathan—"

"It was him," she growled. "Do you know how badly they want to host the summoning?"

"You can't rule out the possibility that there's another adversary—or maybe even two. Those who will just sit tight and wait for Amaraq and Ethesus to destroy each other. If you behave like this, you're doing them a favor."

"I don't care what they want. A bunch of cowards ambushed an old man. If they killed Pukak, I'll tear them to bits…"

"And what? What will you achieve by doing that?" Caedmon asked. "Trying to get yourself killed. That's very mature, Alyna."

"He's right, Alyna. You need to lead Amaraq. No one else can do it."

"I am not a mage. I can't do Amaraq any good."

"You owe me, Alyna. I have never asked anything of you. But now, it's time. I need you." Pukak sat down on the chair behind his desk. A pile of papers on the desk fell to the floor. Alyna bent down to pick them up, trying to do anything to avoid looking at Pukak.

"Come here, Alyna," Pukak said weakly.

She ignored him and continued to pick up the sheets of paper on the floor.

"Alyna!" She felt Caedmon's hand on her shoulder. She stopped what she was doing and looked up at Pukak. The room was so small that when she swiveled around, she was kneeling right next to him. He tilted her face up and looked into her eyes.

"Don't cry, Alyna. You are my family. Amaraq is my life's duty, but you are the only family I've got. If you don't want to take care of Amaraq, it's totally up to you. After I die, you will be free to go and live your life as you wish."

He wiped the tears falling down her cheeks.

"Forgive me, Pukak."

"There is nothing to forgive." He looked up at Caedmon. "It's a shame we met you too late. I regret that I must take Amaraq to the grave with me. But trust me, Caedmon, the business is worthy of your investment. Not because it's profitable, but because in this insane world, when we head toward the end of the third millennium without spiritual guidance, humans will be at a loss. It's not a war between supernaturals and humans.

It's a war between good and evil." He sighed. "Unfortunately, when Amaraq is gone, evil will win."

"How?" Alyna asked.

"The Scorpio key we worship isn't just a key to open sources of power. It's a key that can open the gate that connects the world of good and evil."

"Why is it your responsibility, Pukak?" Caedmon asked. "The world is vast. There are many with power. No insult intended, but Amaraq is merely a small tribe."

Pukak shook his head. "I don't know. It's been like that since the beginning. It was handed down to me. The summoning happens only once every hundred years. Not all leaders have experienced it. I have had a long reign. I've lived long enough. Unfortunately, Amaraq ends with me."

"Don't say that, Pukak!" Alyna cried out.

"You're right, Caedmon. We are only a mage tribe. But protecting the Scorpio key is a mission larger than Amaraq, larger than our lives. I don't know how to handle that…"

He leaned back in the chair and closed his eyes.

"Oh no, please don't leave me. I'm not ready. I'm not made for it. But I'll take the role. I'll lead Amaraq!" Alyna cried.

Pukak opened his eyes. "I don't want you to do anything you might regret."

"I'll do it. Please appoint me."

200

Pukak couldn't sit upright any longer, and Caedmon had to help him. Pukak placed his palm on Alyna's head. But nothing happened.

They waited a little longer, but nothing occurred.

"Is it because I'm not a mage?"

"I can turn you," Pukak said. "I can give you the light, but I'm too weak to do it now."

"Oh no…please don't die. Can you wait for me? I'll be back, Pukak. Promise you'll wait for me."

"I'll try."

She looked at Caedmon.

He nodded. "I'll stay and watch him," he said. "Go. Do what you have to do."

She nodded and stormed out the door. She rushed around the corner, shouting, "Lazi!"

Her gray cat sauntered out from the dark, looking at her as if it knew this moment would come.

"Take me to Teacher."

Lazi turned and ran. She followed right behind.

CHAPTER 30

The cat disappeared in front of Alyna.

It had been taking her to the Teacher. It ran, and she followed right behind it. Then it vanished.

But she kept running in the direction the cat had just vanished from.

She felt as if she had walked past an invisible curtain. She couldn't see anything, but she felt it brush against her. Her skin prickled. Then she found herself standing in front of a temple. There was engraving on the solid steel door and on the walls and fences surrounding the temple. She didn't, however, see any statues representing gods or any other higher power.

Maybe it's not a temple after all, she thought.

The door slid open and then closed behind her after she walked in.

Inside was a large and empty room—dark, smoky, and rather spooky. The air was icy, and she could see her breath. She glanced around but didn't see anything that hinted at the culture, era, or origin of the Teacher.

A distant, authoritative, and disembodied female voice said, "I am pleased to finally see you coming back."

"I'm here to submit myself to you, as promised. What kind of creature will you turn me into?"

There was a chuckle. "You will find out when the power is with you. One thing I can tell you right now is that I will not make you a mage. You will be much more powerful than that. And you will need all of your power to face what is coming. You need to explore your power, and you must use it with care."

"Will I remember anything about my human life?"

"Your human life ended with the car crash. I used a minor form of power to sustain your body until now. Although the power wasn't yours to start with, it has been with you for a long time and has now become an inseparable part of you. So you will feel the same after you receive the new power."

"Can I heal others? Give power to others?"

"Yes, but it will take a long time and a lot of practice before you get to that level. Nevertheless, you will know what to do given different situations."

She nodded.

"Are you ready?"

"Yes, Teacher."

"Kneel. Close your eyes."

She obeyed.

She floated into the nothingness. Oceans of energy flowed into her body. In her mind, the countryside, mountains, rivers, cities, and the faces of several people flashed before her. So many images and faces. She didn't recognize all of them. But among them, she saw Caedmon, and not because he looked different, or because he stood out from the crowd.

She knew he was there for a reason. She wasn't sure if what she had just seen was a flashback, a memory insert, or a projection of the future. But Caedmon's image was so prominent it was ingrained in her mind.

After a while, the process seemed to come to a stop. She opened her eyes and found herself on the floor. She scrambled to her feet. The temple was no longer there, but the voice of Teacher still echoed in the air.

"It has been a great pleasure to give you back your power. Be careful. Don't allow your body to be destroyed again. I will be in touch when it's necessary."

"Wait. What do you mean by giving me back my power?" she asked. But nobody answered.

An empty space of red dirt and industrial ruins surrounded her. Her cat lay sleeping with all four legs in the air, snoring loudly.

"Lazi."

The cat woke and blinked his green eyes at her. He sat up and then leisurely washed himself.

She wasn't sure where she was exactly, but she had some theories. She didn't think she was close to the clinic.

An air motorbike zoomed toward her and hovered. The driver smirked and crooked a finger to wave at her. "Want a ride somewhere to have fun?" he asked. "I tip well. What's your rate?"

She smiled at him. "Sure, I'd love a ride. I'll tell you my rate when we get to where I need to be."

She ran toward the bike, jumped up in the air, and knocked him to the ground. Lazi had settled on the backseat already before she zoomed away. She had no idea he was so fast.

"Pick your bike up in central," she said as she accelerated, heading toward the dome of the city.

She dropped the bike in front of the clinic and raced in. Caedmon was there, and Pukak still sat in the chair. He'd promised he would wait for her, and he had.

Then she saw the expression on Caedmon's face.

"No!"

"He tried. I could have helped if it wasn't poison," Caedmon said.

She darted over to the chair. "You promised me you'd wait. I have power now... I can heal you."

She knew he couldn't hear her. He was somewhere else. He looked as if he were sleeping. Caedmon handed her the shield of the leader, a palm-sized badge that represented the power of the mage tribe.

"Pukak said nobody needs to know you haven't received the proper transfer of leadership. He said he had no power left anyway, so there won't be any proof of the transfer. And you will always have his blessing no matter which way you want to lead Amaraq."

She held up the badge. "We will have proof." She gathered her new energy, injected it into the metal badge, and pressed it to her left forearm until her flesh sizzled.

"What about you, Caedmon? Will you stay to help us? Are you still interested in the business?" She looked at the tattooed imprint on her arm, remaining as aloof and nonchalant as possible. Part of her wanted him to stay, but the other part wanted him to go away.

"I told you I can't get the funds now."

"I don't need the money. But it would mean a great deal to me if you stayed. The trial is next week, and we have so many things to figure out."

"You need to know that I have been approached by Ethesus. They've made an offer to form an alliance."

"Yes, I know. But you came back to me. That's why I asked. Will you stay to help us a little longer?"

Caedmon nodded. "Where do you plan to hold the trial?"

"At the temple. No one needs to know Pukak has passed. I'll announce my leadership position at the temple, before the trial."

"I'll bet there will be resistance."

She nodded. "It might be dangerous. You can decline if you wish."

"I'll be there for you."

"I appreciate it. Could I please have a moment alone with Pukak before we take care of his body?"

Caedmon nodded and exited the room.

She looked at Pukak, who looked to be sleeping peacefully. There had been so many times they'd had discussions in this room. She sat there, looking at him and waiting for his wise words, his guidance, and even his wicked humor about the world before the Great War.

But now, Pukak was no longer talking to her.

CHAPTER 31

Alyna didn't like having butterflies in her stomach. Today was the day of the trial. The senior members from every branch in every corner of the world were coming to Old Sydney to attend. Most of them would stay on for the main event next month. But some would leave early—not all branches and clubs were keen on the ritual.

She hadn't slept at all, so she couldn't really say she'd gotten up early. Lazi had been pacing all night, but mostly because he was nocturnal. What surprised her was the fact that Caedmon had stayed over. He'd told her it was unsafe for him to go back to his apartment because of the attack the other day, but she knew that was only an excuse. He stayed in the guest room, meaning the sofa as she didn't have a spare bedroom.

She tied her hair up and braided a ponytail then put on a leather jacket to cover her tattooed leadership seal. As she came out to the living room, she saw Caedmon was awake. Maybe he hadn't slept, either.

He looked at her with cool eyes that froze any anxiety she was feeling. Approached her, he said, "You'll be fine. You're the rightful leader of Amaraq."

"Thank you for staying. I want you to promise me if things go pear-shaped, you'll leave the temple immediately and not engage in a fight."

The first rays of sunlight beamed through the glass into the room, silhouetting Caedmon and making him look like a dark angel. In her words, he was goddamn beautiful.

"It's a simple request. Agree, or I won't take you to the temple."

"I can't promise you that. But I still need to go to the temple with you."

"Agree, or you'll stay home with the cat. You can't have it all, Caedmon."

She expected him to chuckle. But he didn't. His eyes grew intense. "There's something I need to tell you."

"Does it have to be today?"

He gazed into her eyes. "Yes, and it has to be now."

She nodded.

"One of the things on my agenda is to acquire Amaraq, obtain the Scorpio key, and place it in a secure place."

She stared at him. "Safer than where it currently is in a secret temple of which nobody knows the exact location? Safer than the key making an appearance only once in a century? Where would this secure place that you're talking about be?"

"I can't tell you."

"Well, if you can prove that it is indeed safer for the key to be there than in the temple, let's do it."

He stared at her. "That's it? You agree?"

She arched an eyebrow. "Why not? You obviously have more resources than the hundreds of Amaraq branches combined. Why shouldn't I accept your offer? I don't have Pukak's spiritual appreciation, but I take his word seriously regarding the safety of this world and how the Scorpio key keeps it secure from the invasion of evil. That's his legacy, and I will protect it, whatever it takes."

"You're a good woman, Alyna."

"It's too soon to draw a conclusion like that, Caedmon." She paused. "What are your other agendas?"

"What?"

"You said this is *one* of the things on your agenda. What are the rest?"

He chuckled. "They're not important."

She shrugged. "All right then, let's go."

***

The temple door slid open. Her stomach quivered, and her anxiety was intensifying by the second.

Following her were Caedmon and Tomkin. She knew she could rely on Caedmon in chaotic situations. But she had seen Tomkin countless times in difficult situations, and he simply turned into a mess.

More than a hundred leaders followed her inside. She knew they had many questions for her, but the timing wasn't appropriate, so they held their silence. It worked in her favor, and she was relieved.

It was ice cold inside the temple. Pukak had warned her about this. The temple was made of ice, and the artificial lake in the center of the temple where the key was kept frozen came from a sacred mountain. The frozen water of the lake kept the air in the temple at a frigid temperature.

"Where's Pukak?" Tomkin asked for the second time. Caedmon urged him to remain silent, and Alana pretended not to hear his question.

They approached the lake, and the chill intensified. The leaders climbed onto raised platforms around the lake. The fifty-foot-tall domed ceilings kept the cold air in. It felt as if they were in a freezer.

Alyna looked at the frozen lake. She knew that under the icy surface was the key. She approached the lake and stepped onto the raised platform in the center of the crowd.

"Welcome everyone," she said, "and thank you for attending this summoning trial. For those who don't know, my name is Alyna McCabe. I am Pukak's protege. It is with my deepest sorrow that I inform you Pukak passed away last night due to natural causes. He went peacefully, and he expressed his appreciation for your longtime support of Amaraq. He would also appreciate your continuing support under my leadership in the future."

The room hummed with murmurs.

Alyna removed her jacket, revealing her arm with the leadership seal.

"But you're not a mage!" a male voice cried from a corner of the room.

Alyna turned in his direction. "I am Pukak's protege. You don't think he would have given me the light long time ago?"

"He told me he was concerned that you're not a mage. He worried he'd die without having a successor. He said that to me just last month," a woman at her right said.

"I doubt he'd discuss that with anyone," Alyna replied.

"You don't want us to think you killed him for this leadership post!" someone else said.

"That's a ridiculous accusation," Tomkin said.

She felt Caedmon tugging at her elbow as the room exploded with debates, arguments, conversations. Everyone spoke at the same time, and all of them wanted to be heard. She had special power now, but Alyna knew she hadn't yet had a chance to learn and understand her power, let alone use it. If several senior members of the tribe decided to attack her at the same time, she would be doomed.

CHAPTER 32

Alyna had to reveal her talent and control the situation, or she would never gain respect from these older leaders, Caedmon thought. As much as he wanted to help her, he knew if she didn't act, his involvement would only make things worse.

"Do you want to challenge my leadership by combat?" she asked.

The room quieted down instantly.

"I'll take her!" a male voice responded. A formidable man stepped out from a corner.

Before Alyna could respond, the man attacked her. Every mage had a different talent, but all the talents centered around light energy. Caedmon could see the light energy emanating from the man. As he moved, the light haloed around him. He didn't pull a weapon, but the tenacity in his eyes made Caedmon realize that whatever he had planned would be lethal for Alyna.

He didn't know yet what Alyna's power was, so he stood still and waited. In the worst-case scenario, he was prepared to jump in. As the man came closer, Caedmon switched his eudqi on in full.

Alyna's expression didn't waver a fraction. The man came closer, almost closing the distance between himself and the platform where Alyna, Tomkin, and Caedmon were standing. Alyna waited.

Then she raised her left arm—the one with the leadership seal on the forearm. She made a fist and pushed it through the air. A bolt of light energy emerged from her fist, striking the man like a missile. He was thrown backward like a rag doll and skidded on his backside across the icy floor. His body stopped at the far side of the room, and he lay on the floor, motionless.

"Anyone else?" Alyna asked.

"Yes!" three men cried in unison, running out from the crowd. The trio looked like giant triplets—old men with long white hair wearing long black cloaks.

Alyna charged down the platform in anticipation. A ring of light approached, surrounding her. She raised her arms to grab the ring and started swinging it. The light now looked like a glowing rope with balls of light at both ends. She swung the rope so fast the light looked like a curtain protecting her.

When the trio came closer, she changed the path of the swing, and the rope reached out like a snake, hitting the trio, one by one, across their foreheads. They passed out on the floor before they had a chance to realize what hit them.

She withdrew the light. "Anyone else?" she challenged.

Silence.

"All right, if there are no more objections to my leadership, as a part of this trial ceremony, I'll show you all I am a genuine protege and Pukak's leader by his wishes."

She approached the lake and stepped onto the frozen surface. Feeling the ice was solid, she walked to the middle of the lake. Then she turned and faced the crowd. "We all know what's underneath this icy surface. It is our duty to protect the Scorpio key. It is Pukak's legacy, and I swear with my life to protect it."

She crouched and placed her right palm on the ice. Underneath the ice, something glowed a blinding white.

"Leaders of Amaraq, I present to you the Scorpio key. The key will surface during the summoning ceremony, and you will be able to see the full scope of its magnificence. As for now, rest assured, the key is safe and sound and is under our protection."

The light bounced off the ice and reflected onto Alyna's face. She looked magnificent, Caedmon thought. Was that something mages had in common? Sedna had the same aura when she fought. He shook the thought from his head, deeming it inappropriate to compare his wife and Alyna. As the crowd gasped, Caedmon knew she had gained the leaders' respect. She had earned her leadership.

He felt a movement at his side. Tomkin came from behind him and jumped onto the icy lake. He brandished a knife and stabbed himself in the abdomen. Then he pulled down his outer layer of skin to reveal a metal body underneath.

"Nobody move," Tomkin said. "I'd suggest you all listen to me. I don't want to have to kill you." He turned to look at Caedmon. "You think I didn't know you scanned me with your primitive technology? I gave you the signal you wanted to see." He chuckled.

"What are you?" Alyna asked and started to withdraw the light.

"I told you not to move." Tomkin knocked on his metal body, and it made a hollow, clanking sound. "I'm not a creature. I'm a weapon. Your magic can't kill me, Alyna. And unfortunately, I was sent to blow up this place, along with the Scorpio key and Pukak." He shrugged. "Pukak has died, but you can easily take his place, Alyna."

As Tomkin turned toward her, Caedmon blasted a heatwave at him. But Tomkin was a robot at a much more advanced level than the technology from Caedmon's era. His heatwave had no effect. Tomkin turned toward him.

"It's your fault!" Tomkin said to Caedmon, and he looked as if he was going to blow up the entire temple.

CHAPTER 33

She grinned. The Thunder Child couldn't help but giggle. She had found the way to cut the bloodstone. She used the compound the Teacher had taught her to make to soften the stone.

She had spent days in the woods, high up in the mountains, searching for the rare flower pieces in the ingredient list. Then she processed the flowers carefully. It had taken her a long time to make the compound, only because she didn't have the tools the Keymaster did.

She had a theory. The ice had been created from the Scorpion king's blood. It was not an ordinary stone. He would need to soften the stone first using the blood of an innocent. The Keymaster didn't take her suggestion seriously, and he didn't like her theory, either. So it wouldn't surprise her if he was never able to finish the key.

The Keymaster had spent a long time carving the bloodstone to make the Scorpio key, only to see the stone heal itself and return to its original form. There had been countless failed attempts, so many that she had lost interest in discussing the making of the Scorpio key with him. Or maybe it was the Keymaster who had stopped talking to her. He got like that when he ran into tough clients for whom he couldn't produce the key they wanted or for those he didn't want to make a key for. In any case, he didn't take failing well when it came to his key-making business. And so she had talked to the Teacher to discover ways to solve the Keymaster's problem.

Taking advantage of an opportunity when he was away for a short period of time, Thunder Child collected enough material to make the compound, soften the key, and carve the stone herself. She smiled again, seeing the compound absorbed into the bloodstone and watching the stone sizzle and begin to separate even before her knife cut through it.

***

Caedmon had no choice but to send in his mind blade and cut a gap in the icy surface of the lake beneath Tomkin's feet. He didn't know whether it would work. His mind blade normally worked on a larger scale. He could cut a high-rise in half, for example. But the space in the temple wasn't ideal. He didn't know if he would be able to operate effectively in such a small area.

As he expected, the ice cracked. But not enough for Tomkin to fall through. To ensure Tomkin fell without discharging himself as a bomb, Caedmon jumped over to him, landing as heavily as he could on the ice. He broke a hole through the ice and dragged Tomkin down with him.

"Keep the light on," he said to Alyna on his way down.

He didn't know much about the Amaraq mage tribe. He wasn't sure all mage tribes used their power in the same way. But Sedna had told him that mages couldn't use their warm light effectively under water. So he was sure nobody would be able—or willing—to come down here to give him assistance in dealing with this robot.

He thought it might be the same with his light energy. His newly acquired heatwave talent would most likely not be effective underwater. This fight between him and the advanced robot would have to be one of sheer muscle strength.

Underneath the ice water, Caedmon saw a magnificent fifty-foot-tall ice pillar. Inside the ice was the blood red statue of a scorpion. It stood, encased in ice, staring at him. *That* was the real Scorpio key. Now he knew that what he and Sedna had obtained years ago wasn't the real thing. It looked nothing like this key.

The ice-encrusted scorpion looked like it was bleeding. A stream of red liquid ran from the statue, through the ice, and then into the water. In the water, it dissolved into red bubbles and faded away. The combination of glowing ice, red stone, and bubbling red liquid made the scene both eerie and magnificent at the same time.

Tomkin was mesmerized for a moment by the scale of the ice pillar and the sight of the Scorpio key. Then he shook himself back to reality. He turned, looked at Caedmon, and smirked. Before he could act, however, Caedmon swam over, pulled out a knife, and jabbed it into Tomkin.

He didn't know magic, but he knew robots and technology. He knew how to turn machines on and off, regardless of how advanced the technology was.   At the nape of the robot's neck, a critical switch snapped under the force of Caedmon's knife. Tomkin turned and grabbed for him. Caedmon's eudqi was on in full, so he was extremely careful not to let Tomkin anywhere near his chest. A strike on the chest would be fatal for him. He had to defend his fatal eudqi point at all costs.

They struggled under the water. Even though he'd already had one critical switch destroyed, Tomkin was still strong. Caedmon managed to connect a few strategic hits to nonfatal parts of Tomkin's body. He swung his knife again and struck the robot in the heart area.

No effect. This robot model was more advanced that he had thought. Having a critical switch there would be much too obvious.

Tomkin kicked Caedmon, sending him to the bottom of the lake. Caedmon opened his mouth in surprise, swallowing a mouthful of the icy water. He glanced up to the surface and saw some of the leaders gathered around the hole in the surface of the frozen lake. They were there to help him, he thought. Alyna still kept the light steady for him.

He was running out of air. Apparently, having a super power didn't give him any advantage in breathing underwater. It dawned on him then that Tomkin—as a robot—didn't need to breathe. As if the robot could read his mind, it swam over and grabbed him as he tried to swim to the surface.

Caedmon stabbed Tomkin a few more times, but it didn't help much because none of the attacks seemed to hit the critical switch of the robot. Tomkin dragged Caedmon further down into the depths of the lake. Caedmon knew he didn't have much time left before he drowned.

He turned and stabbed Tomkin in the left eye. The robot stopped moving for a brief second.

Got it! he thought and then stabbed the right eye.

The robot jerked, paused, and finally stopped moving altogether.

It was blindingly unlucky for the robot that its critical switches were in its eyes. Caedmon chuckled inwardly as he kicked his way up to the surface. When he was near, a number of hands reached down to help pull him up and out of the lake. His organs were probably ice by that point. He couldn't even speak.

"Lay him down," someone said.

"Take him out of here," someone else said.

He was brought outside the temple.

"He needs some light," someone else said.

Then Caedmon felt Alyna's hands on his. "Let me," she said.

He switched his eudqi off. It was all he could manage to do. The last time, when Sedna tried to inject him with mage energy, his body had rejected it. He didn't know what kind of energy Alyna had, but he couldn't stop her from giving him the light. His teeth chattered, and his throat was a block of ice. He just closed his eyes and waited.

Soon, he felt warm energy pouring into his body via her hands. He coughed and spat out some water from his lungs. She patted his back. "Toughen up, soldier!" she said and grinned at him then helped him sit up.

An old leader approached. "So you're the LeBlanc guy who wants to take over our business?"

Caedmon coughed a few more times then chuckled. "I can't get the funds now. Can we talk about that later?"

The man grinned. "Sure. You move pretty well for a paper pusher."

"A what?" He coughed a few more times.

"Never mind," the man muttered. "Let me know if you need anything." He looked at Alyna. "This is just the beginning. And I don't think this is Ethesus's doing. They're bikers. They're not high-tech. There's no way they would send a robot to kill us."

"Plus, Ethesus wants to host and protect the Scorpio key, just like us. They wouldn't want to destroy it," Alyna said.

The old leader stood. "See you in a month. There's going to be a showdown with whatever or whoever it is that sent this robot. I'll send help your way, but be prepared—and stay alive. They might want to take us down before the event," he said.

Together, he and all the leaders left.

Alyna wrapped her arm around Caedmon's waist to help him up.

"Come on, Alyna. I can walk myself."

"Well, you should have seen yourself five minutes ago." She smiled and let him walk on his own.

Alyna secured the temple door, and the two of them headed back to her place in the city. Caedmon turned to look at the temple one more time as they walked away. He wasn't a psychic, but he felt the old mage was right. This was just the beginning.

He hadn't planned on all this when he came to Earth. He didn't plan to be involved—to any extent—with the mage business. He had come here to accomplish only two things. One, he wanted to locate the real Scorpio key, and two, he wanted to send someone back in time to swap the real key with the key in the past so that Sedna didn't have to die.

He had achieved neither of his goals. He had violated the fundamental combat principle his father had taught him—avoid fighting while weaknesses are exposed. Humans and magical creatures were too complicated for him to deal with, and they had exposed his multiple weaknesses.

CHAPTER 34

Caedmon sat on the sofa, glaring at Lazi. The cat walked around him, eyeing him up and down, his tail repeatedly swooshing left and right. He liked cats, but this huge gray cat didn't seem to like him at all.

"Is he angry about something? Am I stealing his couch?" he asked when Alyna came back from a round of security checks around the house.

"There's no way you're sleeping on the couch, Caedmon. You take the bedroom, and I'll fix up the training room for myself."

"No, that's not right. I'll stay in the training room…" He stood up, but his legs failed him, and he flopped back down. It became increasingly difficult to breathe and felt as if his lungs were swelling. His mind was growing numb, and he shook his head to clear it. Fatigue took over his body with incredible force and speed.

"You don't look like you could fight even the cat for the couch." Alyna looked at him closely. "I'm taking you to the medical center." She hauled him up. He stood for a few second then dropped back down again.

"Let me sit here for a bit," he said with difficulty and started coughing. Alyna said something, but he couldn't quite hear her.

There was a loud bang at the front of the house. Alyna rushed out to check.

What's going on? Caedmon mentally retraced his steps, starting with the fight at the lake in the temple. He could remember no injuries. Figuring he must have some internal wounds, he switched on his eudqi to heal himself. Whatever it was should be a minor injury. He'd be able to fix the problem quickly. He had done it countless times before.

His eudqi wouldn't switch on.

Don't panic, he thought and tried again.

Nothing.

This had happened once before when Sedna had kicked him in the chest, close to his critical point, when his eudqi was on. In that case, his power was cut off, and he'd almost died.

But he had been extra cautious during the fight with Tomkin. He hadn't let the robot near his chest. And he had no physical wounds at all. Then it dawned on him. He recalled that each time Tomkin hit him, he had gulped some of the lake water. When he'd tried to resurface, without success, and was running out of breath, he had coughed and breathed the water into his lungs.

He didn't know what the Scorpio key was made of, but he knew it was ancient. It had been made way back at the beginning of time. He didn't want to think about what might have been living and growing inside the red statue all that time—and then leaking out into the water in that bubbling red liquid. The same liquid he had breathed in and taken into his body. Maybe it contained a substance—or maybe even a living creature—that his Eudaizian body couldn't handle.

He realized then that the critical point on his chest had been attacked from the *inside*. In the ice water, the viruses and bacteria that Leanne had warned him about had penetrated his system and attacked his fatal eudqi point from inside his chest. He had been totally ignorant of that possibility.

The nonresponsiveness of his eudqi now confirmed his theory.

He could feel darkness invading his mind, and he knew he wouldn't remain lucid for long.

There was a commotion at the front. He looked outside to see Alyna battling a handful of fighters. He couldn't tell how many fighters there were or whether Alyna had the situation under control.

He shook his head to clear his fuzzy mind then went back to the sofa. Every movement he made was like trying to move a mountain. He knew he would die shortly, and right now, his top priority was protecting his wrist unit from falling into an adversary's hands.

He turned on the holocast.

Lorcan looked at him from the screen. "I've been trying to call you Caedmon." He paused. "You look horrid."

"I don't have time to chat, Uncle Lorcan. I've been attacked at my fatal eudqi point—when it was on—by some kind of virus or bacteria…" A round of coughing stopped his speech. When he came back on, Aunty Orla was right next to his uncle. Tears gleamed in her eyes. She was about to say something, but he gestured for silence.

"It's my fault that I'm going to die. There's no remedy for this. Could you please tell my parents I'm sorry… And tell my sisters I'm proud of them and love them. I still can't accept Sedna's death…but if I die now…and I can be with her…wherever she is…please tell my family I died a happy man."

He cut off the holocast and blocked it from further calls and traces. He pulled out his gun and shattered his wrist unit—his only connection with Eudaiz—into hundreds of untraceable pieces.

Then he collapsed onto the sofa and blacked out.

CHAPTER 35

Alyna struck down the last fighter in her front yard and then dragged all of the bodies to the sidewalk. "You're public waste," she told the dead men and returned to the living room.

In the living room, Lazi sat on the sofa, hissing crazily. Caedmon lay on the sofa, unconscious.

"Caedmon." She rushed over and shook his shoulders.

He was cold as ice. She held his hands and injected her light energy into him as she had done before.

A force erupted from him that threw her backward against the far wall. She almost blacked out from the strength of the hit. She was glad she had a hard head. She scrambled back up and raced to the bedroom to grab some blankets.

She wrapped him up.

He was still breathing. Barely. "Caedmon, answer me. You're pissing me off."

She felt a warm rush over her skin. A beam of light appeared in the middle of the room. She pointed the gun at two human shapes that started to materialize. She would have shot them had they not given her a gesture of peace. They completely materialized into a beautiful, young human couple.

The woman rushed out of the light beam and darted toward Caedmon.

"Stop! Don't touch him, or I'll shoot!" Alyna shouted.

"Don't shoot. I'm Lorcan, and that's my wife, Orla. Caedmon called us Uncle and Aunty. We're not blood-related, but we're really close. He called us just a few minutes ago to give his last words to his family before he died. We just want to take him home."

"What? No, he's not dead."

"But he's dying," Lorcan said. "In case you don't know, we're from another universe. Caedmon has supernatural power, but he has a weak point on his chest.

He said it was attacked by a virus in the lake—and that it's fatal."

"I can fix him!" Orla said. Tears rolled down her face, and her eyes were red.

"No, Orla, no. I know he wouldn't allow you to do that. If you use dark magic on him, he'll resent you for the rest of his life."

"Surviving with dark magic is better than being dead. You're a living example, Lorcan."

"It was different back then, Orla. Remember the price we paid for using dark magic? You don't want that for him."

"I don't want him dead, either."

"Before I brought you here, you promised me you wouldn't do anything drastic, Orla!"

"If I didn't tell you that, would you have taken me with you? Did you think I just wanted to come here to collect his body? Do you really think that, Lorcan?"

"Save your domestic disputes for home. He's not dead yet. You are in *my* home, and he is *my* guest. Now get away from him, or I *will* shoot you." Alyna brandished her gun.

Lorcan pulled Orla away from Caedmon. "We just want to bring him home. He has a mother and a father and two sisters. They deserve to know where he is and what happened."

"Let me repeat, he's my guest, he's not dead, and I didn't invite you into in my home. Now go!"

Orla looked at her. She had never seen a woman so beautiful and exotically mysterious. "I'm a sorceress. I can bring him back now. Please let me!"

"Using dark magic? I wouldn't want that if I were him," Alyna said.

Orla shook her head. "But you hardly know him. His wife was a mage. He is open to magic."

"Where is she then? If she's a mage, why isn't she doing anything for him?"

"She died," Orla said.

"Oh…I'm sorry."

"Caedmon might be open to magical creatures because Sedna is a mage. But he was never open to sorcery," Lorcan said.

"I'll fix him. Please go. You're wasting my time," Alyna said.

"How will you fix him?" Orla asked.

"Not with sorcery. That's all you need to know."

"Are you a mage?" Orla asked.

"No, but I know what I'm doing. Now you really need to go. There's one thing I cannot do—I can't bring him back from death."

"If you turned him into something other than what he is now, his family might object to it," Lorcan said.

"My name is Alyna McCabe. I am the leader of Amaraq. I will save his life and will use whatever means I deem acceptable and necessary. If his family has any objections, you know where to find me." She fired into the wall next to where Orla stood. "Now please go before I cause some real damage."

"If you can't save him and he dies, we reserve the right to take his body back home. He won't be buried on Earth."

"We aren't burying anyone here. Trust me."

Lorcan and Oral withdrew to the light beam, and they, along with the beam, vanished.

CHAPTER 36

Alyna darted back to Caedmon. His body had grown colder, and his lips had turned purple. She stroked his forehead, brushing a stray lock of hair aside. "You can hate me for doing this, Caedmon. But you'll have to be alive to do so."

Lazi walked back and forth, hissing again. His fur stood on end as if jolted by an electric current. Alyna looked at the cat.

"Is the Teacher here?" she asked. "I guess that's a yes from you."

She held Caedmon's hand and squeezed it lightly. She knew he would feel her presence. Then she said, "Teacher, I'm calling you. You gave me one privilege. I'm taking it now. Please come to me."

The light in the room darkened a shade. And then the Teacher's voice, distant, said, "I've been watching you. I know what you want to do."

"Then please save him, Teacher."

"He has to give consent, just the way you did when I saved you from the car crash."

"He's in no condition to consent to anything right now. But I am giving consent on his behalf."

"It doesn't work that way, Alyna. I don't do anything for nothing. If I save him, and he then says he never asked for the privilege, it won't be good for me. I must profit from each soul I trade."

"Take my soul. Take it as my trade. This privilege will be my debt to you. You can call on me for anything in the future."

"Are you sure about this?"

"He doesn't have much time left. He fought for the mage tribe at the temple, and he saved me when we were complete strangers."

"You are still strangers now! Do you really know him at all? Do you know his family other than by reputation?"

"He is a compassionate man. I'm sure it will be worthwhile for you do this. Please!"

"He might object to what he will become for this second chance at life. He might not like the creature I turn him into. This action cannot be reversed."

"Do you know what you'll turn him into?"

"No, not yet. It depends on his make and his willingness to accept the new form. Given that he can't demonstrate his willingness, I'll take your word instead. What do you think he would want to be turned into?"

"I don't even know what you have made *me*. If I'm allowed to make a request for him, can you make him into the same kind of creature you've made me?"

"You're a very special kind of shapeshifter, Alyna. He certainly has the make for it. But do you think he would want that?"

"Anything is better than death, Teacher."

"Okay. But do you know how strong he is? He's even stronger than you are. You're saving him and facing a lifetime of debt for him. But if, later on, you and he part ways for any reason, and you're on opposing sides, you will lose to him in battle."

"I'll kill him before he has a chance to become my opponent, Teacher."

"That's my student! I knew you were the right one when I chose you. Now turn around, and close your eyes."

She obeyed.

She felt warmth on her skin and heard the gentle sound of chanting in the distance, as if echoing in from the darkness. But she knew her Teacher never used dark magic.

It was the right decision. She was sure of it.

The chanting subsided.

"It's done. Remember, you owe me for this one, Alyna."

Then the light vanished.

Alyna turned around and saw Lazi staring at her. "What?"

The cat said nothing, which didn't surprise her. He stood up on all fours, sauntered over to the sofa, jumped up, and started licking Caedmon's face.

Caedmon winced. "Get that rough tongue away from my face!"

She rushed over and sat on the sofa next to him. "Hey, stranger!"

"What happened?" he asked.

"You tell me."

He sat up. "We fought at the temple. I went into the lake. It was cold beyond imagination. I terminated the robot, Tomkin. Then…"

"Then what? You don't remember?"

"Then it was cold."

"You said that."

He squeezed his temples.

"All right, let me help. The old leaders provided the energy to warm you up because you were nearly frozen. Then you passed out. I took you home."

"You took me home? You mean, you carried me?"

"Yeah, on my shoulders. I'm very strong. Wanna try me?" She stood, patting her shoulders and tilting her body as if she could carry him piggyback.

He laughed. "No way."

She smiled. "We called a cab, of course, you silly. You slept for a while. Are you feeling okay?"

"Yes, perfect actually. So what will happen next month? We organize the real deal at the temple?"

"Yes, but we have to be careful. The older leaders think Ethesus isn't likely to send robots. So in that case, we're dealing with an unknown enemy."

Caedmon nodded. "I told you I met Nathan. He didn't look like the kind of guy who would use robots. But he didn't look like he was into spooky elusive matter, either."

"What do you mean by that?"

"Well, things like magic and magical creatures. I don't do well with paranormal things. I can handle technology, but when it comes to vampires, werewolves, and angels, I'm at a loss."

"But you wanted to take over a mage operating business. I thought you were open to those things."

"Just because I'm open to them doesn't mean I want to deal with them or approve of the way they operate. My sister is different. She's curious about the paranormal world. She studies it. But not me."

She chuckled. "What if you turned into a werewolf one day?"

He laughed. "That's not possible. Vampires bite people and turn them into vampires. Same with werewolves, I think."

"They do it with consent. Same with mages. You have to give consent to receive the light."

"But it's totally unnatural. You're either born to be something, or you're not. Turning into something paranormal is off limits for me."

Lazi purred and climbed onto Caedmon's lap. "Why are you suddenly liking me so much, furry buddy?" He scratched the cat's neck. It closed its eyes and purred louder.

"Traitor! He wanted me to do that for him yesterday," Alyna said and stood. "I'm starving. I'm going to grab something to eat."

"Yes, please. I feel like meat. Something raw." He shook his head. "I can't believe I just said that. I don't like raw meat. But I'll go with you." He put the cat down on the floor.

"Let's go," he said, opening the door for her like a gentleman. "You never know, I might grow some fangs tomorrow."

"Not funny."

"What? Now you're sharing my odd feelings about the paranormal?"

THE MULTIVERSE COLLECTION

BLOODSTONE TRILOGY
PREQUEL

ASH OF SCORPIO

BY
D. N. LEO
USA BEST SELLING AUTHOR

CHAPTER 1

Winter 2065 in Greenland was as cold and miserable as the last twenty-nine winters she had experienced. But this one was special. This winter, Sedna wouldn't be just a mage. If things went as planned, she would become the leader of her tribe. She didn't know how big of an *if* it was. But she would just have to deal with it as it came to her.

She squinted, looking more carefully at the golden sculpture of a scorpion. She had thought it would be much bigger than this, but it was just slightly larger than her palm. The eyes of the scorpion flashed like fire. She shook her head and blinked. When she looked again, the eyes were back to normal. She sighed. She had averaged three hours of sleep a day in the last two weeks. It obviously had consequences.

Afton had been training her for over a year now to ready her for the leadership. Her combat skills and her ability to control her energy as a mage had improved a lot. He said she was now ready to take what was rightfully hers.

This scorpion sculpture was the first step toward the power.

The shiny golden sculpture of a scorpion with a ring of diamonds wrapped around its neck stared back at her. She was a professional picker, and she'd been making a good living from it. She had a knack for valuable artifacts—she knew their worth, their authenticity, and most importantly, their potential profits.

Something was wrong with this sculpture. If it was a fake, it was a damn good one. But Afton wouldn't use unreliable sources of information.

She turned around to look at the well-dressed man waiting patiently next to her. "This looks interesting, Mr. Quinn. I need to make a phone call."

Mr. Quinn nodded and exited the room.

Sedna pulled out her phone. "I'm unsure about this one. But it looks authentic."

"Looking authentic isn't enough, Sedna. I need you to know with certainty. We can't afford to make a mistake."

"Afton, if you make me choose, I'd say it's real. I'm a damn good picker, and I've been doing this for years. The only reason I'm not sure about this one is that my gut is telling me there's something wrong."

"So apart from your gut feelings, your professional judgment about the item is that it's authentic?"

Sedna sighed. "Yes, I would say so."

"Well, that's good enough for me."

"You shouldn't trust me so much," she mumbled.

"What?"

"Nothing."

She hung up the phone. Mr. Quinn entered the room and approached Sedna, waiting for an answer. She looked at him and said, "All right, I like what I see. I'll go talk to my boss, and we'll arrange a place for the exchange."

She returned for a last look at the sculpture. She supposed her gut feelings didn't qualify as suspicion. They needed this merchandise. She snorted softly at the way Afton called it *merchandise*.

Why should he disguise the fact that they were going for the leadership of the tribe? As far as she was concerned, her mage tribe was fair and righteous. She would be the rightful leader if she lived up to it. And Afton supported her. That was all that counted.

But before she could say anything further to Mr. Quinn, she heard the muffled sound of a gunshot, and a bullet pierced through the glass window, so hard and fast that it punctured the glass without breaking the entire window.

Blood and brains splattered both her and the sculpture of the scorpion. Someone had shot the old man. The bullet had pierced his skull from the left temple to the right.

She ducked to the floor just before a bullet hit the cabinet behind where her head had been. She reached up and grabbed the sculpture then scrambled on all fours across the floor. More bullets whizzed through the room, hitting the furniture.

She pushed the side door open and raced across the slippery, snowy backyard.

Damnit! She had parked her car in the front. She started to turn around, but bullets sprayed in her direction again. Trying to get to the front was a stupid move. She turned back around and darted through the snow of the dark national park. She dialed Afton, putting her phone on hands-free so she could talk while she ran.

She could hear footsteps behind her.

More bullets.

Her own footsteps.

She ran.

And ran.

Afton picked up the phone.

"Someone shot at me!" she shouted.

"Where are you?"

"Outside. I can't go back to the car."

"Take cover somewhere. I'll send Anatole to get you."

She ducked as bullets sprayed next to her and punched holes in a nearby fence.

"Take cover, goddammit!" Afton shouted.

"I can't. They'll catch me."

"Do you have the merchandise with you?"

"Yes."

"Jesus Christ, that's what they're after. Throw it away."

"But..."

A bullet hit her shoulder. She fell to the snow. The scorpion sculpture dropped to the ground and spun several feet away.

"I dropped it..."

"Are you hit?"

"Yes. I dropped the merchandise."

"Goddammit! Leave it. Run. I want you back here alive, Sedna."

She hung up the phone and ran. Turning back, she could see a shadow dart at the sculpture. She wanted to keep running. Afton had told her to run. But they had worked for months to get here. She couldn't let some coward with a gun scare her.

She stopped running.

The person wore a robe, a hood covering his head, making his face even darker in the night. *Not your typical assassin's outfit,* Sedna thought. He held the sculpture in his hand and stared at her with inhuman piercing green eyes that tore through the darkness.

He stared at her for a moment and then raised his gun, aiming at her.

CHAPTER 2

Caedmon held his breath. One more slot, and he would be free from the transformation chamber. He smiled. *Slot. Such a term shouldn't be used on Earth,* he reminded himself. Last time, Uncle Tadgh had helped him with the conversion between Eudaizian time and Earth time. The distance between Eudaiz and Earth was a twisted maze of metaphysical elements and couldn't be measured in typical time and space dimensions.

Caedmon almost laughed out loud when he recalled the look of disdain on Uncle

Tadgh's face when he mentioned this description. In spite of being a mathematical genius, Uncle Tadgh disliked anything that sounded too complicated or formal.

A slot in Eudaiz was equal to either several minutes or hours on Earth. But numbers weren't Caedmon's friends, so he had forgotten again. Not everyone had to be a walking, talking computer like Uncle Tadgh. Even Caedmon's father had to check his wrist unit whenever he needed a conversion.

His parents, Uncle Tadgh, and everyone else on the council were humans and had come from Earth. But he hadn't. He'd been born here. So it was a steep learning curve for him even regarding such trivial issues as human behavior on Earth. But he was a quick learner.

The glass door of the opposite chamber opened. Caedmon opened his eyes and saw his father. He straightened himself up quickly. He had passed through three stages of the dimensional transformation chamber, and his father couldn't get in here.

Caedmon looked at his father. People said Ciaran LeBlanc was the most prominent powerhouse in the cosmos, the most formidable man. They also said Caedmon would be the spitting image of his father when he grew up—and he was grown up now. He hoped he wouldn't disappoint.

"Caedmon, you don't have my permission to time travel. It's dangerous, and the technology is still unstable," Ciaran said.

"I just want to help, Father."

"Then go back to your future and stay there."

"You're in charge of a universe of more than six hundred billion citizens. I'm only trying to help you. As your son, it's the least I can do. I'm not a fragile piece of crystal, you know."

"I have many important matters to see to, but instead I'm standing here negotiating with you. How is that helpful, Caedmon?"

"You'll fail this mission, Father."

"I beg your pardon!"

"I'm sorry to have to tell you that. But remember, I'm from the future, Father. I've seen the records. You will fail to obtain the Scorpio key."

"Jesus Christ, Caedmon! What have you done? You can't change the past. If I fail this mission, then so be it. You can't change it."

"Don't you want to know what happened after Hoyt Flanagan beat you to the key?"

Ciaran braced his hands against the control panel in his compartment and looked down. Then he looked back up at Caedmon. "No, I don't want to know."

"You're being selfish, Father. You're worrying about me and what might happen if I get tangled up with the time travel."

"I'm your father. I have the right to be selfish—"

Caedmon cut in, "Hoyt pulled out the temporary shield you put in to replace the missing Scorpio key. And that sank the entire Arctic, caused massive floods, and killed half the population on Earth. Do you still not want to know what happened next, Father?"

His father looked at him. Caedmon swore he could see tears in his eyes. He knew he was pushing the right buttons. So he pressed on.

"I have a solution, Father. I can get the Scorpio key for you."

Ciaran paused for a long moment, and then he asked, "How?"

Caedmon drew in a breath. "I hacked your system, and I found out that the failure was due to a mage tribe in Greenland. So I traveled to Earth to see what they were all about and why they had caused this mission to fail."

Ciaran cocked an eyebrow "And did you find the answers you were looking for?"

"No. But I think I know how to fix it."

Ciaran narrowed his eyes.

Caedmon continued, "I met someone in the mage tribe. I can approach that person for more information."

"You met someone? Are you insane? When you time travel, you're not supposed to cause sequential changes..." Ciaran trailed off then took a deep breath to calm himself down. "When did you travel?"

"Yesterday."

"What was your Earth age?"

"Thirty."

Ciaran shook his head and sighed.

Caedmon continued, "It was a good contact. I'm sure I can get more information if

I go back. And I know all about the issues with time traveling, Father. I'll try my best not to cause significant changes. But there's no other way. You tried and failed. You can't go back and fix it. But I wasn't involved. I can."

Ciaran nodded. "Who was the acquaintance?"

"Actually, it was a little more than an acquaintance. I met a girl. A woman, I mean. We emotionally engaged."

Silence.

"'Emotionally engaged'...what do you mean by that?"

"We...like...we did a lot of talking. I liked her. A lot. And I think she liked me, too..."

"Did you have sex with her?"

"Father! No, I didn't... Okay, yes."

He saw his father's jawline harden as he braced his hands on the glass wall and closed his eyes.

"Father, I'm sorry."

"Did you say anything to her before you came back?"

Caedmon shook his head.

"So now you plan to go back to her. From yesterday to today, Eudaizian time, do you know what the time gap is on Earth?"

Caedmon shook his head again.

Ciaran said, "It's been four years. You had a relationship with a woman, and you disappeared without explanation. You're going to show up after four years, still without a good reason. Do you know how she is going to react?"

"Based on my analysis, she'll have a negative reaction that might result in tears and mild violence, given her personality traits. And she might initially object to my approach due to distrust. Am I correct?" Caedmon asked, raising his eyebrow in anticipation of a positive response from his father.

Ciaran shook his head. "In a word, son, on Earth, they'd say she'd be pissed off."

"Say what?"

"Never mind. You're smart. You can deal with that. The problem is, in Eudaiz, people only know righteousness. You're a Eudaizian ..."

"You're human. That makes *me* human," he cut in.

"That's debatable. You don't know Earth. More importantly, you don't know human, Caedmon. Your Earth knowledge and experiences are computer generated. You'll be disadvantage when you fight humans."

"There won't be a fight..."

Ciaran stared at him. "All right, you *really* need combat experiences. I'll load these experiences to your profile. Digest them and make them truly yours. However, if you have to make quick decision when dealing with humans, remember one thing - trust no one. Now, place your right palm on the control panel."

"Oh, no. Dad, I haven't done anything to qualify that—"

"I can't let you go on a mission unarmed. I'm giving you the eudqi."

He was receiving the Silver Blood that everyone talked about. Never in his wildest dreams did he think he could get it — the most powerful energy and weapon in Eudaiz. He obeyed his father and placed his palm on the control panel. His father entered a series of commands and codes into the computer from the other side of the glass wall.

A burst of energy came into his body. It flooded his system. His body and mind floated. It felt as if he had disintegrated and then reassembled. He felt an inexplicable flow of blood and energy through his body.

Power.

"Your eudqi critical point is on your chest, toward the right. That is your weakest point. If you're attacked there when you have your eudqi on, it will be fatal. If you have your eudqi off when you are injured, your eudqi will heal almost all of your injuries very quickly. So think carefully before you use this energy source."

Caedmon nodded. "Thank you, Father."

"When you come back, you will be a commander."

"Father!"

"When you land, try to hold off the action for as long as you can. I'll send help your way. But because I haven't planned this, I'm not sure who to send. Can you promise to think carefully before doing anything drastic?

"Father, I—"

"Can you follow orders? Do you understand the implications of not following protocols?"

"Yes."

Ciaran nodded. "Go now."

He looked at his father one last time and then turned on his heel.

CHAPTER 3

Sedna could smell the stench of fresh blood from the man as he approached. He still pointed the gun at her. She cursed the fact that she was unarmed. She wasn't arrogant. She just hadn't thought she'd need a gun to visit a client.

"You've got what you wanted. I don't have anything else with me," she said. Blood seeped from the bullet wound on her shoulder. Her vision started to blur.

The man still approached. "Sedna Aardel?" he croaked.

She could heal her wound, but she really needed to rest to do so. At the moment, with only half her brain functioning properly, she knew admitting to the name would be unwise. "Who?" she said.

The man frowned. "You're Sedna Aardel," he repeated.

"I don't know who you're talking about." She inched a bit farther from the man to give herself enough space to strike. *Damn, Afton.* All of her training had focused on defense. And now, in this situation, she didn't know how to attack a man. The fact that he had a gun on her didn't help, either.

"Okay, I lied. I'm not Sedna Aardel, but I know where she is."

The man cocked an eyebrow, considering.

Not very smart, are you? she thought.

"Where?"

"You're pointing a gun at me. If I tell you, I'm sure you'll go ahead and shoot me."

He nodded and lowered his gun. Taking the opportunity, she charged at the man for a tackle. Not a wise idea. His body was as hard as rock. Her shoulder cried out in searing pain. She felt she was going to pass out.

She couldn't let that happen.

The man staggered back a few steps and smirked. He slid the sculpture into his pocket and holstered his gun.

Great. She followed with a roundhouse kick, the back of her foot impacting with his face. He smiled like she intrigued him. *Oh shit.*

He walked slowly toward her. She felt as if she was pounding a brick wall. *Is he a creature? He certainly isn't human.* That much she knew. No matter how much she punched and kicked him or how much energy she used to strike him, he kept walking toward her, intact.

She hit him again and again. And she could tell it wasn't going to work.

It was too late to run as he would shoot her in the back. She swung one last kick. He grabbed her foot. His hand was like a pair of iron pliers. One twist of his hand, and her leg would be torn flesh and shattered bones.

She yanked hard. To her surprise, she freed herself from his grip. She lost her balance and fell on her backside, skidding over the snow.

The man growled and charged at her. She kicked her feet at the snow, pushing herself away and sliding backward. She didn't have enough energy to get up and run.

"You know what I'm going to do to you, bitch? Call Afton—he can come and collect your body after I'm done with you."

"Who are you?"

Her world started to fade. The man smirked and advanced on her. She couldn't let it end like this. She gathered the last drop of her strength and pumped a two-leg kick at his groin.

He roared.

But that was all of the damage she could do. She dropped back down to the snow. The man hunched over and charged at her.

Suddenly, he stopped in his tracks. From behind her, beams of light struck the man. He staggered. He roared and looked as if he was on fire.

"Afton!" she said.

A shadow walked past her then darted straight at the man, piercing a dagger through him from his front to his back. It was no ordinary dagger. And the man wasn't Afton.

That was her last thought before her world went black.

CHAPTER 4

Caedmon dampened a towel in warm water and went back to the bed where he had put Sedna. He cleaned the mud and blood from her face. She looked the same as he remembered her. Of course, in Eudaizian time, it was only yesterday that they had been intimate.

As his father had mentioned, he wasn't sure how things had changed in the four years of Earth time that had passed or whether she would remember him. Father had said she would be *pissed* at him. He hadn't had a chance to look up the meaning of the word, but he got the impression it wasn't a good thing.

The Scorpio key would be at the temple where they appointed leadership of the mage tribe. The key would only reveal itself when the scorpion sculpture activated it. Then the sculpture has to be placed in a shield plate, and remain there, because its removal would cause a gigantic astronomical hole that would sink the Arctic. So the upcoming leader of the mage tribe would have to relinquish the sculpture, and thus, the power, so Caedmon could remove the Scorpio key and get out safely.

His father seemed to think it wasn't possible to ask a human—in this case, a creature on Earth, a mage—to give up the power he had fought a lifetime to gain to save a multiverse that most humans and creatures didn't even know existed.

The technology in Eudaiz was advanced by several hundred years compared to Earth. The transformation machine basically created beings to desirable specifications. It sampled his natural biological and psychological profile and simulated a version of him in the time and space of his choice, and then loaded the necessary experiences to his profile so that he could operate in the new environment. So the simulated Caedmon was uniquely him.

The machine was the creation of which his father was most proud. The technology had been initiated several hundred years ago, but it hadn't been completed until his father's time.

Caedmon had loaded his human profile when he met Sedna, and thus he was a human to her. He would tell her his true identity someday, but not now, not while he was on this mission. There was too much at stake. And aside from what his father thought, he understood the implications of not following protocols—he would never let his sentiments jeopardize the mission.

The tribe had to trust him enough to let him in. That way, he could be there when they took the sculpture to the temple. To gain their trust, he had to either be one of them or be a helpful human. The fact that he was from another universe would never gain trust from the mage tribe.

Once inside the temple, he had to obtain the sculpture, get the key, and lock the sculpture in place to permanently shield the hole.

Sedna stirred. Her eyes fluttered. She opened her eyes and stared at him.

Caedmon squirmed. He was still unsure about the magnitude of the expression *pissed off*, but he forgot his fear when he saw her wince in pain. He rushed over to the bedside.

"Hey! How are you feeling?" He tucked her long, black hair back, revealing her beautiful oval face, dark eyes, and full red lips. "I know it hurts. I'm sorry I didn't come sooner. It was incredible how you pushed the bullet out of your shoulder!"

He didn't react quickly enough, and her hand contacted his face. He saw stars and tasted blood in his mouth. Now he knew what his father had meant by that expression.

Sedna sat straight up in bed. "Don't touch me, you bastard!" she snarled.

Caedmon stepped back and switched his eudqi on. His mind worked like a computer as it translated: 'A bastard is a person born of parents who are not married to each other.'

That's not right, he thought. *My parents are married.* But he chalked the comment up to Sedna being angry at him.

"Sedna, I can explain. But you have to calm down. You're injured. You have to rest." He approached her again.

"Who do you think you are? You just wanted to sleep with me. As soon as you got what you want, you took off. Now you try to come back playing hero! Why? You want more sex?"

"I said I can explain it, Sedna—"

"I don't want your explanation. Let me guess—you're going to tell me you didn't intend for us to be intimate. You were attracted to me, and things got out of hand. Then something important happened, and you had to leave without even saying goodbye. And now you're back with an explanation for everything, hoping to get into my pants again."

"Th-that about sums it up. Except for the getting into your pants part. That wasn't my intention."

"Oh, so you didn't even plan to come back? If that creature hadn't been about to blow my head off, you wouldn't even have stopped by to see me?"

He moved closer to the bed. "That didn't come out right. I mean—"

She stood and swung a kick at him. The moment the heel of that pretty foot landed on his chest, his world exploded.

He staggered backward. He couldn't breathe. His vision wavered. Pain spread through his chest like a flash flood.

What had his father said? The critical point of his eudqi was on the right side of his chest. If he was hit at that point, the blow would be lethal. He had turned on his eudqi to use his mind's eye to access the database, and he had left it on. Was this the end? He hadn't even begun his mission.

His knees buckled. He saw Sedna reaching out to hold his shoulders. "Caedmon, I'm sorry. I didn't think I kicked you that hard. Look at me, Caedmon... Come on..."

He saw her concerned face. And maybe even some tears. And then he couldn't see anything.

CHAPTER 5

Afton searched the area frantically. "Sedna!" he called out, although he knew that was a stupid thing to do. Fear stabbed at him. He said he'd send Anatole to go after her, but Anatole was a contract killer—an assassin who killed for a living.

When it came to Sedna's safety, he trusted no one but himself. It had been a mistake to send her to see the client on her own. Her stubbornness aside, he should have been more insistent about her taking bodyguards with her. The day of the leadership contest was coming close, and this round would be brutal. The power hungry would have sent out assassins. After more than a hundred years of being a mage, he should have known better.

He knew he was at the scene where the incident had taken place. Afton crouched. There was a trace of blood and gore right here. But it wasn't Sedna's. By the looks of it, whoever had spilled blood here couldn't possibly be alive. *But if Sedna killed the assassin, where is she?*

And then he saw the sculpture, broken in half. *It was fake!* He shook his head.

The falling snow didn't work in his favor, but he was a damn good tracker. He looked around and saw some tracks. He was sure they were from Sedna. Afton concentrated and looked harder. He saw a second set of tracks. There had been someone else here. He ran his fingers over the imprints in the snow. He sniffed to try to pick up the scent.

This was very unusual. It was something he hadn't come across before. Sedna's tracks ended, but the second set went on. Afton checked to be sure his weapons were in place, then he followed the trail.

***

Sedna shook Caedmon's shoulders. He was breathing, but he didn't respond. He didn't look like he was dying. She shook him again. His eyes fluttered and opened slightly.

"Caedmon, can you hear me? Can you get up? I'll get you to the hospital."

"No. Just let me lie here for a slot. I'll be fine," he said then passed out again.

"A *slot?*" she asked then realized he hadn't heard her question.

It was strange, but then again, she was used to strange languages. She was the last line of her Alaskan tribe in Greenland. She spoke some Eskaleut, but she didn't use it for communication. There weren't many people around to warrant the use of the language. It was useful mainly to read old manuscripts.

Let me lie here for a slot, he had said. *What the hell does that mean?* It didn't really matter, though. What mattered was that he was injured. She was a mage, and she could heal him. She opened the front of his shirt and admired the defined muscles of his chest. She shook her inappropriate thoughts out of her mind and concentrated on her healing. She had kicked him on the right side. She couldn't see a bruise, but the blow had apparently hurt him nevertheless.

She focused, placing her palm on the spot where she thought the injury was. There was a spark of light. She felt as though she was being electrocuted. The vibration was so strong it numbed half of her body and shot her back several feet. Her head hit against the wall, and she blacked out.

After a while, she opened her eyes and sat up groggily. She rubbed the back of her head. "What the hell? What kind of a creature are you, Caedmon?" she asked out loud. But he was out of it, and she didn't expect a response. His body had rejected her light. *How strange.*

She would have to let Caedmon heal himself. She fetched a blanket and tucked it around him. She brushed the hair out of his face and took a long look at him. It had been four years since she'd last seen him. She didn't want to admit it, but she couldn't get the last night they'd had together out of her mind. Since then, she hadn't been able to...well, never mind. She sighed.

He looked the same but a few years older. Time had worked in his favor.

She was sure he had reasons for leaving. But whether she would listen to him and allow him back into her life now remained to be seen. A lot of things had happened in those four years. She was now moving toward becoming the leader of her tribe.

Back then, it was different. She had been carefree. She'd had her own life, and she had been in love with Caedmon. Back then, it had been her cousin who was going to lead the tribe. But then he had died in an accident two years ago, and the tribe reached out to her. Afton took her in for training, and one thing led to another. Now here she was, unsure about whether she could have a normal love life ever again.

Thinking of Afton, her head perked up. *Shit!* She should call him. *Where is the bloody cell phone?* She searched around the room and couldn't find it. *Damn!*

Then she sensed him. It was the connection between trainer and trainee. She assumed it was a merely a professional connection, but whenever she sensed him around, she always felt as if she were a kid about to get caught sneaking lollipops to bed. Like she hadn't been working hard enough and hadn't been doing her homework.

Sedna whirled around. She knew Afton was coming for her.

She shivered.

Afton hated scholars, and when he said he hated something, he meant it.

When she first met Caedmon, he was a college boy from Oxford University, a British scholar researching Native American culture. She hung on his every word. He had incredible knowledge, and he was sexy as hell.

She had never planned to tell Afton about Caedmon. Not back then. And absolutely not now.

Caedmon was still on the floor, unconscious.

She heard Afton's footsteps. They were the sort of footsteps that most people wouldn't be able to hear because he walked like a cat.

But her mind's ears, if there were such things, must have been attuned.

"Sedna!" Afton's voice came through the door. This time, her human ears heard him. She darted over to Caedmon and pushed him under the bed.

She tidied her hair and yanked open the door.

"Afton!" she grinned. But he didn't smile back.

CHAPTER 6

Nikki finished polishing the nail on her left little finger and gave all the nails a gentle blow of air. She looked at her beautifully manicured nails and smiled. Although she had put only a sheen of an almost transparent silver dust color on them, the nail polish made a world of difference to her look.

The only girl on this planet who would leave her nails plain because of martial arts practice was her friend Sedna. Nikki shook her head. No wonder Sedna had never had a boyfriend. They'd been friends for a long time, and she knew Sedna was a mage. Sedna had introduced her to the tribe and had been the one who'd recommended her for this job.

They needed a human to manage the natural medicine clinic—someone who could understand the tribe, be discreet, and handle problems caused by humans. As this was the only natural medicine clinic in Nuuk—the capital of Greenland run by creatures—they anticipated a number of problems caused by their human fellows. The most sustainable solution was to have a human on staff.

This clinic was the main training ground of the contenders for the upcoming leadership. There had originally been twelve candidates. After several rounds of competition, however, there were only three left—Sedna, Neva, and Keeve. But only Neva and Keeve trained here. Sedna practiced at Afton's exclusive martial arts hub.

Nikki felt her day brighten as Keeve walked in. He looked at her with his striking blue eyes. They didn't talk much to each other, but his eyes were always warm. "Hi, Keeve. You're early today."

"I'm not practicing today. I just left something in my locker," he said and pointed to the changing room.

"All right then."

As he turned down the hallway to the changing room, she pulled out an invitation and put it on the counter. When Keeve came back out, she called, "Keeve!"

"Yes, Nikki?"

"This is to thank you for the fishing trip last week."

"It was my pleasure. We had a good time, didn't we?"

"We did." She pushed the invitation across the counter.

Keeve looked at it. "Jazz?" He raised an eyebrow.

"You don't like jazz?"

"I love it."

She grinned. "They're a local band. Opening day."

"We should support the locals, shouldn't we?" He smiled at her. "Thanks. See you next week."

When he turned to leave, she asked, "Is it a date?"

He slowed down and turned around. Those blue eyes grew pensive, and she hated that. "You know we can't, right?"

"Why not? So what if I'm human and you're a mage."

"It won't work."

"Says who?"

"I need to think about this..." His voice trailed off, and he turned around and walked out of the clinic.

Nikki didn't know how long she stood there, staring at the door. She swallowed the lump in her throat when she saw Anatole bolt into the reception room.

"Sedna's in trouble. Do you know what's going on? Afton called to tell me, but then he just cut me off and didn't say anything else," Anatole blurted out before checking to see if Nikki was paying attention or even cared what he was saying.

Nikki arched an eyebrow. "And you came here to ask me because?"

Anatole leaned in close, glanced around, and lowered his voice. "Have Neva and Keeve been using the training room?"

"They aren't stupid, Anatole. If they wanted to hurt Sedna, they would send someone to do that and show up for practice as usual."

Anatole nodded. "Sorry. You're right. I overreacted."

Nikki rolled her eyes. "I'm surprised!"

"Come on, cut me some slack. Their leadership challenge is coming soon. I'm a little tense, okay?"

Nikki clucked her tongue. "It's not *their* leadership challenge, it's Sedna's. You couldn't care less about Keeve and Neva."

"I thought you guys were friends. Which camp are you in, Nikki?" Anatole tugged absently at the side of his jacket. Nikki knew well that there was an arsenal in the lining of that jacket—special weapons used especially for assassination jobs.

"I'm a business manager—I don't take sides. All members of the tribe who use this venue are my clients."

"Put your New York manner away. Nuuk is a small town."

"Too small, I'm afraid. Everyone knows everyone else's business."

Anatole shifted his stance. "What do you mean?"

"Two men came here yesterday. They were asking to join the training club. I knew they had sniffed around and found out this clinic belonged to a mage tribe. I told them we sell natural medicines and offer no training, but they left unconvinced."

Anatole narrowed his eyes. "What did they want exactly?"

"I think they wanted to see a mage in training."

"And when did they come?"

"Just before I closed for the day."

"That's actually at night."

"Well, if you're thinking they were vampires, I didn't see any fangs."

Anatole shook his head. "Well, if they weren't hunters, they had to be paranormal creatures of some kind."

Nikki waved her arms in the air. "How would I know? If Sedna hadn't told me she was a mage when I caught her drawing energy from the sunlight, I would have never been able to tell. But judging by what they wore, I'm sure they aren't locals."

Anatole nodded. "That's good enough," he muttered and started to walk away.

"Where are you going?"

"If they aren't locals, that narrows things down a lot. Again, just in case you don't know this after being here for two years, Nuuk is a small town."

She saw him smirk before he turned around again, and she asked, "You're not going to do anything to incriminate the tribe, are you?"

Anatole stopped in his tracks. "Incrimination by which law?"

"Greenland's criminal justice system! That's not good enough for you?"

Anatole laughed. "Yep. It's good enough for a law-abiding citizen of Greenland." Then he pushed open the door and left. Nikki frowned. She knew Anatole didn't abide by the law. She weighed her options and then picked up the phone to call Afton. Before she had finished dialing, Moss walked in.

Moss was a mage. He looked to be in his late fifties, but Nikki knew he was more than a hundred years old. In terms of power, he was of the same caliber as Afton. He had originally wanted to train Sedna, but Afton beat him to it, so he took Neva, who, in Nikki's opinion, had no chance against Sedna.

As Moss cast a glance at her, she could see the anger in his eyes and could smell the blood on his breath. She was willing to bet that the rumor about him eating children for breakfast was real, and that was why Sedna hadn't picked him as a mentor.

"What did Anatole want?" Moss asked as he moved closer to her. His proximity was too close for her comfort. He peered down at her, waiting for an answer.

If he got angry and attacked her, Nikki didn't think her manicured nails would serve very well as weapons. "He..."

"Why are you hesitating? Did he want something you can't tell me?"

"It has nothing to do with the tribe."

"Really? Then tell me."

"He...he asked me out. Is that against the tribe's policies?"

Moss arched an eyebrow. Then he grabbed her hips to hold her in place. His fingers dug into her flesh. "Let me tell you something, young lady. I know you've been spying on us for Afton and Sedna. I know you think Neva isn't good enough to win the challenge. But this isn't about Neva. It's about me. And the good news is that Afton has never beaten me. Never. If he thought he stood a chance against me, he wouldn't need a spy."

He shoved Nikki to the wall and strode toward the long hallway, heading for the training room.

CHAPTER 7

Caedmon opened his eyes. He could feel the cold hard floor underneath him, and the ceiling seemed to be right above his face. Was he lying on the floor in a basement crawl space? Was he in a box? Where was he, and why would he in a box? He tried to clear his mind and think, but everything was a blur. Then he heard Sedna's voice and a deep male voice. He blinked. The male voice didn't sound friendly, and whoever it belonged to appeared to be questioning Sedna. They couldn't be in the same room as he was because their voices seemed to echo in from a distance.

He blinked and concentrated again. The fog in his mind gradually lifted. He felt a surge of energy, and he knew it was the Silver Blood kicking in to heal his injury. His mind cleared even more quickly. He recalled he had switched his eudqi on to access the database, leaving the Silver Blood on. Sedna must have contacted him close to his fatal point.

Idiot, he scolded himself. Father had said he had to be very careful when he used the power. This was his first serious lesson. If the kick had been a couple of inches further to the right, it would have been his last lesson. He flexed his muscles. His system was healing fast and was already about eighty percent complete.

"Don't lie to me, Sedna," the male voice scolded.

Is Sedna in trouble? He tried to recall what had happened in the room, but nothing else came to mind. Then he felt hands grab at his legs. He was only eighty-five percent healed, but it would have to be good enough. He switched his eudqi off. Immediately, he felt the disadvantage of being an injured human—he was weak. The hands gripped at his legs tighter and pulled him out from under what he now realized was a bed.

As he sat up groggily, Sedna darted over to help him. She tried to shove the man who had pulled him out away.

"He's harmless, and I injured him, Afton," Sedna said sternly.

"If he's harmless, why did you hide him under the bed?"

"He's my friend, and I didn't know how you would react seeing him in my room. He saved me from the bastard who stole the sculpture."

"On that note, I'm sure your friend isn't human. A human can't kill that assassin." The man Sedna called Afton approached him. He pushed Sedna aside. He didn't like the idea she was protecting him, and he saw an opportunity to approach the tribe. He wagered this man had significant rank given Sedna had shown respect to him.

"I had help. I have a special weapon," Caedmon said.

"Really?" Afton raised an eyebrow, and as fast as lightning, he landed a punch in his abdomen. Sedna squealed some profanity, and

Caedmon slumped to the floor and heaved. The punch was so hard it made him nauseated. He was tempted to switched his eudqi on but refrained from doing so. His second lesson of the day was that being human sucked when it came to a fight.

Afton shoved Sedna away and pulled Caedmon up to his feet. "I don't believe you. If you're this helpless, how did you kill that assassin?" Afton cocked his arm began to throw another punch, but Caedmon grabbed his fist in its track.

"I didn't return the punch because Sedna respects you. But don't test my patience. I killed that man because if I hadn't, he'd have killed Sedna. He had a gun, and I had a dagger. I considered it a fair fight." He pushed Afton away.

"What special help did you have? What weapon?"

Caedmon went to the chair where his jacket covered his dagger. He held up the weapon made of special Eudaizian steel. The blade vibrated with energy. Afton frowned at the dagger and reached out his hand.

Caedmon pulled the dagger out of Afton's reach.

"Can't I see it?" Afton asked.

"No. I don't know you, and you just hit me. Do you really expect me to give you the only weapon I've got? I'm not an idiot."

Afton glanced at Sedna then back at Caedmon. "Do you trust her?" he pointed at Sedna.

Caedmon smiled. "That's not relevant. We used to be friends. But I left, and now she doesn't trust me anymore. So it doesn't really matter whether or not I trust her."

"Why did you come back?" Sedna asked.

Caedmon shook his head. "It's a long story. Family business. I'm looking for an antique artifact in Nuuk. I recalled it's your expertise, so I thought I'd find you to pick your brain about it."

"What kind of artifact?" Afton asked.

Caedmon gave Afton a stern stare. "Why would I tell you?"

Afton shifted his stance and approached Caedmon. He raised his hand toward him.

"I know a mage like you has supernatural powers. But you haven't felt the power of my dagger. And I'd hate to use it in front of Sedna given her respect for you. Anyway, she's safe and sound now. So if you'll excuse me, I have things to do." He looked at Sedna. "It was good to see you again, Sedna." Then he turned to exit the room.

***

Caedmon walked as quickly as possible. He needed to get to a hotel in Nuuk where his father's commander had placed two human agents for him should he need help. Once there, he could wait for his father to send in a real commander. He hoped it would be Roy. Roy was cool-headed and had been to Earth several times on different missions. He loved to see Roy shift. He was a half-wolf, half-fox were-creature and now resided in Eudaiz. Now, with Silver Blood inside him, Roy shifted into a magnificent space creature.

Well, he realized he couldn't ask for too much. He had caught his father off guard and unprepared. He wasn't sure how many resources his father could gather together in a short time.

Nuuk was more crowded than he remembered it. Four years must be a long time on Earth. Caedmon veered off the main road and walked along a back street. The snow-covered backyards didn't give him any comfort. It was eerie, and he didn't like the feel of the area, so he turned back to the main roads. He thought maybe he should just use a map. He raised his left arm to turn his wrist unit on only to find he no longer had it.

The only device he had brought from Eudaiz, the only technological connection he had, was no longer with him. The wrist unit was everything in Eudaiz. It carried a person's personal profile and connected that person to his universe. It was a life and death matter in Eudaiz—and even more so here, on Earth.

He felt a chill run up his spine. He had never in his life felt so isolated from his people.

The wrist unit must have fallen off when he was under the bed. He had to go back for it. But before he made it too far, he heard footsteps behind him. Someone or something was running toward him.

He checked his dagger to ensure it was ready. If he had to fight now, he would have to fight as a human. If the tribe discovered he was from another universe, they wouldn't let him get close to the temple that held the key.

CHAPTER 8

The picturesque scene of a snowy, sleepy town in popular fiction was a big fat lie. Neva cursed as she struggled to run on the path covered with thick, slippery snow. She supposed she could stop and beat the hell out of the two creatures chasing her. Her training was good enough to defend herself. But if there were more than two, she'd be in trouble. And she had no idea what kind of creatures were following her.

As Moss always said, run first and fight only when absolutely necessary. Moss's best asset to her as a trainer was his wise advice.

He couldn't give her much martial arts training because her capabilities were limited. But she had beaten all other candidates to date except for Sedna and Keeve. She thought she was a true contender for this leadership.

Through the curtain of snow, she saw a man walk in front of her. "Get out of my way!" she shouted, but it was too close to avoid the collision. The man was a decent size, so running into him bounced her several feet away. She fell on her backside, skidding on the snow.

"Are you okay?" The man rushed over to help her up.

"Get away from me," she said as she scrambled up from the ground. If there were more than two creatures after her, there was no guarantee she could guard herself, let alone protect this human bystander. And the tribe was extremely conservative when it came to interactions with humans.

The footsteps got closer, and to her disappointment, there were three creatures in the form of men approaching her. And they were not only men, they were *huge* men. They looked like bouncers at a nightclub.

"Oh shit!" she muttered.

"Are they after you?" the man standing next to her asked.

"Yes, they're after me. But this is none of your business. Run. I can't guarantee your safety." She shoved him away and charged at the three creatures.

They stopped in their tracks when they saw her coming at them. They had expected her to run, and she had. But now she was on the offense, and they didn't know what to do.

All she needed was one moment of hesitation. She pulled the two curved knives tucked in her knee-high boots and advanced. But as she got closer to the men, she started to regret it. She was skilled with knives, but fighting these three gorillas at once might be a very bad idea.

One approached her and pulled a long knife from his jacket—as if his size wasn't enough to give him an advantage over her. He swung the knife and ran at her. She anticipated the worst. She had received a lot of training in martial arts, but most of her fights to date were in contests with other mages in the tribe.

Her confidence wavered a bit, but she continued to charge at the man. She swung her right knife over her head and then stabbed in a downward motion. The man lifted his long knife to block and opened his body to her. She kicked her foot as hard as she could into his groin and followed with the left knife, stabbing into his abdomen.

He roared and staggered back. Black liquid poured out of the wound. He slumped to the snow. His eye socket sparked a greenish-blue light. His body melted instantly, and he turned into a pile of scrap metal.

"What the hell?" she cried.

The remaining men roared. They flexed their hands, and their fingers turned into long, sharp blades. They stormed at her. She took several steps back to figure out a better way to take the two of them at once. There were no ideal solutions.

Then a soft material brushed against her as the human bystander ran past her toward the creatures, a dagger in his hand. She grinned and followed him. She took one creature, and he took the other one. She used the same technique she had used before, but the creature didn't seem to learn from the fatal example from his friend. She killed him quickly and easily. And just like the other one, he dropped to the ground and turned disintegrated into a pile of metal.

She turned around and saw her new friend examining the remains of the creature he'd dispatched.

Am I really slower than a human? If so, she thought, she should quit this leadership contest.

She approached her benefactor. "Thank you," she said. "Your skills are impressive."

The man turned around and smiled at her. Her stomach quivered. He was gorgeous with striking gray eyes and the face of a dark angel. And his smile—he could trademark it. "As are yours." He stood and held his hand out. "I'm Caedmon."

"Neva," she responded then saw a stream of blood running down his left arm. "You're hurt. Let me see."

He looked at the gash on his arm and shrugged. "It's just a flesh wound."

"It's bleeding quite a bit." She grabbed his arm and pulled it toward her. "I'm a mage. I can heal your injury. I have the light, a sort of energy I draw from sunlight."

"I know what a mage can do. But save your energy. I can fix this with a bandage."

"You'll need more than that. It's a large cut. You're injured because of me. I'll feel better if you let me heal you."

Caedmon nodded. "All right then."

"You're very strong for a human," she said and then concentrated, raising her palm and hovering it above his wound. But before anything happened, she heard Sedna yelling, "Stop!"

She turned to her left and saw Sedna and Afton running toward her and Caedmon.

CHAPTER 9

The hotel was quiet, as if the staff had cleared out all bystanders so that he could do his job. Anatole sneaked into a long hallway. This was the third hotel he had searched. There were many in Nuuk, but only a handful would accommodate customers that had anything to do with the paranormal world.

He'd checked the guest list and was sure the two staying in the executive suite were those Nikki had mentioned. He sauntered up to the door and knocked. A man in his late twenties answered. He was much too young to be a hunter. And too earthly to be a paranormal creature. Anatole doubted his previous speculation. They may just be genuine curious tourists.

"Yes, can I help you?" the young man said with a strong South African accent.

Anatole was much taller than the man, and he peeked inside the room without difficulty. There was no one else inside. "I'm from the natural medicine clinic. I was told you were after some training yesterday."

"Yes, but the receptionist said they don't offer martial arts training."

"No, they don't. But I do. I work freelance. I offer private training."

The man looked Anatole up and down.

"Is there a particular reason you want to receive training at that clinic? I have my own studio."

The man shook his head. "No. No particular reason."

"Pizza delivery!" The second man appeared at the end of the corridor with a pizza box in his hand.

"He's a private martial arts trainer," the first man told him. "The clinic referred him because we had asked yesterday."

"All right!" The second man grinned. "Come on in. Have a piece, and we'll talk."

Anatole walked into the room. He had to admit the pizza smelled delicious.

***

"What's your problem?" Neva growled.

Sedna zeroed in on the bleeding wound on Caedmon's arm. She had been sure Caedmon wasn't human when she tried to heal him in the hotel room. And she didn't know what would happen if Neva tried to heal his wound. Not that she minded that he wasn't human. But he probably didn't know she knew, so he had lied to Afton. If they figured it out now, Afton wouldn't take it lightly.

Judging by the look on his face, she knew Caedmon didn't realize she had figured out he wasn't human. Sedna cleared her throat. "A wound like that takes a lot of energy to heal. The contest is coming close. I don't want you to be disadvantaged, Neva."

It was a lame excuse, but surprisingly, Neva seemed moved by it. "Thank you for being fair."

"I told her it was only a flesh wound," Caedmon said and shrugged off Neva's hold. He stanched the blood with his hand. "Having two fights in a day is too much for my liking. I'm going to head to a hotel and rest."

"I'll heal you," Afton said.

"What?" asked Sedna. "No. He said it's nothing. He can get it patched up at the clinic. There's no need for us to flash our mage badge right in the middle of the town."

Caedmon nodded a goodbye to everyone and headed on his way.

Afton darted forward and grabbed Caedmon's shoulder from behind. "I said I would heal you."

Caedmon shrugged his hand off. "No, thank you." When Caedmon turned to walk away, Afton grabbed his shoulder again and pulled him backward. He kicked Caedmon's legs out from behind. Losing his balance, Caedmon landed on his back on the ground. Afton pressed a foot on Caedmon's left shoulder to pin him in place.

"Afton!" Sedna protested, but Afton raised his hand to ask for her silence. Caedmon swung his legs in an attempt to gain some ground. To Sedna's surprise, Neva darted over and jumped on Caedmon, using her weight to help hold him down on the ground. She grabbed his head, holding it with both hands.

"Oh, hell!" Sedna muttered. Neva's unique talent was that she could hypnotize a human in a second. And Caedmon wasn't human. Sedna closed her eyes and waited for Neva's scream. But nothing seemed to happen. She opened her eyes and saw Caedmon knocked out in the snow as if it were the most comfortable bed in the world. His head was cradled in Neva's hands, and Afton was healing him. It was going smoothly as his healing process always did.

"What is your real name?" Afton asked.

"Caedmon LeBlanc."

Neva and Sedna looked on.

"What are you here for?" Afton asked again.

"The key," Caedmon said.

"Afton, he didn't agree to any of this!" Sedna objected.

"She's right, Afton," Neva said.

"Does the key have anything to do with the tribe leadership?" Afton continued.

"Afton!" Sedna exclaimed. "Neva, stop this!"

"No," Caedmon said.

"That's good enough. He's very strong for a human," he said. Sedna rolled her eyes. "You can let him go, Neva," He picked up Caedmon's dagger and examined it with admiration.

Neva gently lay Caedmon's head on the ground. Caedmon opened his eyes. He was groggy at first, then he focused and registered what was happening around him. He sprang to his feet and glanced at his healed wound. By the look on his face, Sedna didn't think he was at all grateful.

"What did you do to me?" he growled.

"You're welcome," Afton said.

"I didn't ask for a favor. Give me back my dagger." He snatched the dagger from Afton's hand and tucked it away.

Afton smiled. "I'm glad you're human."

"If I had fangs, I swear I'd suck all of your blood out." He threw a resentful look at Sedna and walked away.

That look hurt. She darted after him. "I didn't do anything. In fact, I tried to stop them."

"I respect your privacy, Sedna. But your people invaded mine. I didn't agree to be hypnotized."

"I would never do that to you. But it's a critical time for us. We have to be very cautious. Please understand that, Caedmon."

He turned and looked at her. "No, I don't understand. There are only two types of beings regardless what kind of creatures they are—good ones and bad ones. What gives you the right to pry into someone's identity? To look into someone's mind? Humans or creatures, why does it matter?" He glanced at Afton. "Do you think a mage is above all other creatures?"

"No. I never said that. Never for a single moment did I think that," she said. But the look in his eyes told her he was no longer listening to her.

"I regret having come back," he said then turned and walked away—the same way he had walked into the fog four years ago.

CHAPTER 10

Caedmon walked into the hotel where the two agents were waiting for him. There was no time to get back to the other hotel for his missing wrist unit before this meeting, but luckily, he remembered the address. He did plan to get his unit back but wasn't sure he wanted to see Sedna. She might not come back to the hotel room anyway after he had walked out on her—again.

It had been too good of an opportunity to leave her, and he couldn't pass on it. Now she'd hate him, but it'd be better that way. He might be gaining a foothold in her tribe. He didn't want her to be his sacrificial lamb.

"Good evening, may I help you, sir?" the receptionist asked and smiled at him.

Before he could respond, there was a scream from upstairs. Everyone in the lobby of the hotel stopped what they were doing. The receptionist rushed up the stairs, and Caedmon followed. A man who might have been the hotel manager darted out of an office at the corner of the hallway and ran upstairs after them.

A woman in her forties who was wearing a room service uniform raced down the hallway, her face streaked with tears. The blood had drained from her face, and she was babbling something incoherent. But she was pointing toward the open room at the end of the hall.

Caedmon and the manager rushed toward the room. Caedmon was steps behind the manager, who was speechless when he saw what was inside. In front of them, two severed heads had been placed in an empty pizza box which rested on a table.

Caedmon knew who they were. He didn't need to search for information or ask the manager. He knew. He had just killed two creatures today, but that was nothing compared to what he saw displayed in front of him. Now he understood what his father had said—losing men in battle was worse than death. These dead men weren't his people, but they had been sent here to help him.

***

Sedna picked up her belongings and glanced quickly around the hotel room to make sure she didn't leave anything behind. Caedmon had put all of her things on the table, so it was easy to pack. She yanked open the door and nearly jumped out of her skin. "Jesus Christ, Anatole!"

Anatole stood in the hall, leaning against the wall opposite the door to her room. "Ready to go?"

"Since when does Afton think I need a bodyguard?"

"Since whatever happened that made you end up in this hotel with that guy."

"Caedmon isn't just any guy. He saved my ass."

"I'm sure he did more than just saving it," he said.

"Excuse me?"

Anatole looked at Sedna. "Afton said there is a chemistry between you and him. I'm not stupid. I can read between the lines. And to repeat what I said—I bet he did more than save your pretty backside."

She narrowed her eyes. "If he did, why would that be your problem?"

Anatole shrugged. "I despise those who use women to get a foothold in things."

He wrapped his arm around her shoulders protectively. She pushed him away. "Caedmon didn't want anything to do the tribe. In fact, he left this afternoon," she said.

"Yeah. I heard. I'm sorry to hear that." He lifted her chin and saw the gleaming tears in her eyes. "Love bites, doesn't it?" he said, his voice low.

"I'm not sure it was love. I just wish we had parted on better terms."

"Well, his loss."

A tear rolled down her face. Anatole wiped it away then he pulled her into his arms. It had been a long time since she'd needed a shoulder to lean on. So long that she couldn't remember. He felt warm and safe. For the first time in her life, Sedna felt protected. So she leaned in.

After a moment, Anatole said, "Let's get you home."

***

Caedmon had hidden behind the door to the exit stairwell. He looked through the keyhole again and could see that Anatole and Sedna had gone. He'd heard their conversation and had seen Sedna's tears. Whatever it was that he was feeling was unpleasant. He could stand there and analyze his emotional reaction right now, but he set that plan away because he had more important tasks at hand. He waited for a moment more and then pushed the exit door open to go back to the hotel room.

He searched under the bed for his wrist unit. But he found nothing.

He scrambled up from the floor and looked around. It was gone. If it wasn't here, though, where would it be?

Then he saw the handkerchief Sedna had left behind, tangled in with the sheet on the bed. It wasn't just any handkerchief—it was the one he bought her.

He picked it up. The subtle pattern stared up at him from his palm. He shoved it into his pocket. His chest hurt. He didn't know what it was. Maybe it was lingering pain from where Sedna's foot had hit and almost killed him. He shook the distracting thoughts out of his head. He was on a mission. *Concentrate*, he scolded himself.

Before he continued searching for the wrist unit in the remaining part of the room, the door opened. The man standing there was Anatole. "You must be Caedmon?"

"Yes. And you are?"

"Anatole. Sedna forgot something..." Anatole glanced at the rumpled sheet on the bed.

"Forgot what?" Caedmon asked, shoving his hands into his pockets and feeling the silk of the handkerchief.

Anatole flipped the sheet and the blanket over, looked, then shrugged. "Maybe she didn't leave it here."

"Where is she?"

Anatole gave him a stern stare. "It's none of your concern. You left her this afternoon, remember?" Anatole pulled out a pack of cigarettes and picked out one using his lips. He lit it and threw the disposable lighter into the bin. He took a drag and looked at Caedmon through the smoke.

"I know what it feels like. But let me give you some advice from a fellow human. A mage and a human can't possibly last. It was smart that you walked away."

Caedmon nodded.

Anatole continued, "I'm her bodyguard, so this is your fair warning. Don't hang around Sedna and the tribe. The next time I run into you, it won't be so peaceful."

"I left her this afternoon. Why do you think I'd want to linger?"

Anatole smirked. "Experience." Then he turned and left the room.

Caedmon darted over to the trash can and picked up the disposable lighter. As he predicted, it was from the hotel where his agents had been killed.

Caedmon's head spun with fury. Part of him wanted to rush out into the corridor and cut Anatole into pieces. The calmer part of him continued the search for his wrist unit, the only way he could contact his home in Eudaiz.

CHAPTER 11

Sedna felt empty. It would have been easier if Caedmon had never come back. The fact that he had—and then had left her again—was unbearably painful. She had doubted her purpose in life for the last four years. Her life hadn't been exciting before Caedmon, but she got by. She had graduated at the top of her class in anthology and history at Arizona State University. She had a knack for antique and valuable items. She could stay and work in the US, but she had gone back to Greenland. She'd never forgotten her ancestors, her tribe, and the fact that she was a mage. She could never have a normal human life.

Then came Caedmon. Charming. Smart. Sinfully handsome. And most importantly, he made her realize that she could have a life beyond her tribe. A life elsewhere with an identity of her choice. He made her fall in love.

And then he had vanished like a puff of smoke.

Before she knew it, she had started the training and was on the leadership track. It had given her life a purpose. *But now what?*

She flipped through her files and looked at a trail she had planned to follow before she got to this client and things went south. An artifact was due to be delivered to a private collection in the middle of Nuuk. This private collector was a mysterious character. He'd arrived at Nuuk a year ago with a blank background. It made no sense. It wasn't possible that a collector with wealth at that level would have a history she couldn't track.

She shuffled through the files and the photos again. In a corner of a picture, something caught her eye. She picked up the phone, dialed, and heard Nikki's chirpy greeting from the clinic.

"Nikki, it's me. Remember the photos you gave me regarding a new collector in town?"

"Yes, of course. Afton still hasn't paid me for those."

"I'm sorry. I'll remind him. You have the electronic files. Could you have the left corner of photo number twelve enhanced and let me know what you see? You took those pictures yourself, didn't you?"

"Let me see. Hmm…I took the first ten. So number twelve, no. I got my guy to do it. But I have the files and I'll do what you asked. I'll call you back."

***

Caedmon strode along a path just outside of a snow-covered park. It was hard to imagine this was the middle of the town. It was eerily quiet. In the distance, he saw a man wearing a black leather jacket and cowboy boots, sitting on a bench. He looked so out of place that it was impossible not to notice him.

Caedmon approached. "The receptionist gave me a note saying you have something that belongs to me," Caedmon said.

The man looked up at him, leaned back on the bench, and smiled. "I do indeed."

"What do you want to give me?"

"What kind of creature are you?"

"I don't know what you mean," Caedmon said.

"Don't play dumb. That piece of equipment isn't from Earth."

Caedmon laughed. "You mean my watch is alien technology?"

"If it's just a watch, why are you so desperate to find it?"

Caedmon narrowed his eyes. "It's just a watch. My father gave it to me, and it has sentimental value. If you want it, keep it."

He began to walk away.

"Wait!" the man called out.

"I don't like being blackmailed. If you want money, you aren't going to get any from me."

"My name is Keeve, and I'm a contender for leadership of my tribe. I followed Sedna—"

"You stalked her?"

"Look, we're in competition to find the sculpture and win the contest. I can win the martial arts contest if it's a fair fight. But I don't have the resources Afton and Moss have."

"Why do you think I care about any of this?"

"I followed Sedna and saw her in trouble with an assassin. You saved her. The move you made isn't human."

"You'd let her be killed, and yet you expect a fair fight at the leadership contest?" Caedmon exclaimed.

"It's not what you think. Someone attacked me from behind, and I was seriously injured. When I got up, I saw you'd killed the creature. I could barely move at that point. After I healed myself, I followed a trail and found you both in a hotel room, unconscious."

"Both of us?"

"Yes, both of you. Afton was coming, so I yanked the odd watch off your wrist and ran. In this competition, I'm a loner. I have no friends and no mentor. But I've made it this far. I am not prepared to lose if Neva and Sedna cheat."

"Still, why is this my problem?"

"I think you care for Sedna. She's half-hearted about this. It's supposed to be a three-way race, but it'll be easier for me and less dangerous for her if she withdraws."

"And you think I can talk to her into withdrawing?"

"We thought because there are three of us left in this competition, only the three of us want to find the scorpion sculpture. But no. I've been contacted for a contract on Sedna's head and the sculpture in return for a lot of money. I turned the offer down. But there's no guarantee Neva and Moss wouldn't pick it up."

"Who tried to contract you?"

"I didn't have direct contact."

"You said you were attacked. Maybe it was because you turned the offer down. But why didn't they kill you?" Caedmon asked.

Keeve shook his head. "I wondered the same thing. They need the competition to happen. Nobody knows where the sculpture is or who has it. At the final fight between two contenders, whoever has the sculpture will reveal it, and that will give the person triple points for the contest. So if they kill me and then Sedna, then clearly the leadership will belong to Neva without a fight. And she might not have the sculpture. If they kill Sedna, then—"

"All right, all right, I can see the picture. Nobody knows anything about the sculpture, and someone is playing games with all of you."

Keeve nodded.

"I can talk to Sedna, but there's no guarantee she'll listen. Can I have my watch back now?"

He held out the wrist unit. Caedmon snatched it from him.

"Just out of curiosity," Keeve asked. "What kind of creature are you? If I meant any harm, I could have killed you both in the hotel room."

"I'm human, you idiot. A human with some funky technological gadgets," Caedmon said and walked away. As soon as he snapped it on, the wrist unit activated and verified him. A message flashed up with the address of the Scorpio sculpture's location.

CHAPTER 12

Nikki hung up the phone and scrambled toward the desk to pack up the pictures and computer disks she'd left scattered around.

The bells at the door sang. *Sedna couldn't be that fast.* She looked up and saw she was right—it wasn't Sedna at the door. A tall man in a hoodie charged at her. She swung her handbag at him. She hit him furiously and continuously as the contents of her bag fell out and onto the ground.

The man tried to grab her but couldn't because of her flailing arms and swinging bag.

Keep that up, she told herself. She kept pummeling him, withdrawing toward the door as she did so. But before she could reach it, she felt the sharp blade of a knife invade her chest. She looked down to see lots of blood flowing from her as the man in the hood dropped to all fours and shuffled through the contents of her bag.

Nikki lay on the ground, recalling bits and pieces of her life. The visions flew past as if a black and white movie played in slow motion in her mind. She'd lived a good life. She had friends and family. She was happy.

Then the brightest star in her life came in—Keeve. He charged at the man who had stolen her life with one quick stab of his knife. Soon after, she saw the man drop dead on the floor.

Then she felt the warmth of Keeve's body—the energy of a mage. But she knew it was too late. She heard him begging her to stay with him, but she knew her natural life had ended. She didn't know how a mage's energy worked, but there was one thing she did know—they couldn't bring someone back from death, and she had been halfway there.

She didn't want to waste the last moment she had with him. "Whatever it is that you're doing, please stop," she told him.

"Shhh, don't talk. I'll fix you. Let me heal you."

"It's too late, Keeve. Let me look at you."

She could feel his body shaking with emotion, but he obeyed. He eased her out of his arms so she could look at his face. He was beautiful. Those striking blue eyes were always so pensive. Always thinking. He had never taken life for granted. But there was nothing he could do for her human life. "Sedna asked me to look at a photo I had taken for her... I enhanced the image, and I saw Moss' reflection in a corner. He was...stalking a new collector in town. He knew the address. And considering what just happened, I think the man had the scorpion sculpture."

"Please stop talking, Nikki. I don't care anymore."

"You do care. You're a good man. A righteous mage. You should be the leader."

"I don't care. Let me heal you."

"I'm sorry I can't be there to see that...day..."

"Please don't leave me, Nikki."

"I love you, Keeve..." And then darkness claimed her.

***

Sedna ran as fast as she could. The path from the parking lot to the clinic had never seemed so long before. She wasn't a psychic. She didn't have a sixth sense. But her instincts were telling her that something bad was happening to Nikki.

She stormed into the clinic and found Nikki dead in Keeve's arms. There was another body in the middle of the floor. Tears streamed down Sedna's face. It was her fault. She had gotten her friend killed.

She crouched in front of Keeve. He withdrew, snatching Nikki out of her reach. She had never seen Keeve so devastated. She didn't know there had been anything between her friend and Keeve—her competition.

"She told me she loved me." A tear rolled down Keeve's cheek. It wasn't the first time she had seen a man cry, but this was Keeve—one of the most cool-headed and toughest men she had ever come across.

"She's gone, Keeve. We can't bring her back from death."

"It was too fast. I didn't have a chance to tell her I love her."

Sedna touched Keeve's shoulder, but he shrugged her off. He gathered Nikki's body in his arms and walked out of the clinic.

CHAPTER 13

Caedmon snarled at the wrist unit and tried a second time. He was in his hotel room, but if the signals didn't work here, he might have to go outside. But this time, the unit flashed an engaged signal. In a short moment, his father's face appeared on the screen. "I thought Eudaiz technology was unbreakable, Father," he said.

"It's not the technology, it's your unit. Someone other than you has been in possession of it for more than six hours Earth time, and it's about to self-destruct. I was about to send an army down there for search and rescue. Where have you been, and what have you done?"

"I'm sorry."

"Don't be. I just need you to get yourself back here in one piece," Ciaran fumed.

"I'm sorry, Father. When I got here, Sedna was being attacked. I had to take action. Then things kept getting worse. What would you have done if you were me?"

Ciaran rubbed his eyes and leaned back in his chair. Caedmon felt a pang of guilt. It was the first time he had seen circles under his father's eyes.

"Listen, son, you have to stay put. I need more time. There's a problem here I need to take care of, and it's urgent. I wanted to send Roy or your Uncle Tadgh to assist you, but they're both on an inter-dimensional mission and can't get back here right away. I've got a report saying the two agents they sent to you were killed."

"Yes, I am sorry about that."

"Stop saying you're sorry, Caedmon. You're on a mission. It's a dangerous battle, and there will be sacrifices. People will die. That's the reality of combat. You asked for it.

So be prepared. I need you to buy me some time to gather resources."

"Yes, Father. The unit has just flashed me the location for the scorpion sculpture. Should I go get it?"

"Only a mage can tell if it's the right one. There's no point in you going there."

Caedmon nodded. "The Silver Blood empowers an individual's unique talent—like you and your mind blades. But I don't have any talent. So it can only make me stronger, right?"

"How can you be so sure you don't have a talent?"

"Well, you wielded your mind blades for the first time when you were four, and you dug out an entire hillside. I can't do anything like that."

"If I have to guess, I'd think your talent would be something similar to mine just because you're my son, but maybe it'll be in a different form. You'll have to figure it out for yourself."

Caedmon nodded. "So how does that explain why my twin sister's only talent is making cupcakes?"

Ciaran laughed. It made Caedmon feel less guilty. "Lyla's talent is versatile. You haven't seen the full scope of it yet. The fact that she can make cupcakes and you can't should make you question your narrow definition of talent."

Caedmon smiled. "I'll give it some thought, and I'll try to look for my hidden talent."

"All right. Goodbye, son. Stay tough."

When his father's image disappeared from the screen, Caedmon stared at his wrist unit for a long time. His father could wield gigantic steel blades in his mind and destroy any target he wanted. What would his talent be?

He concentrated, focused on the coffee table in the middle of the room, and thought of a small metal plate, like a small fan. He felt a puff of wind blow into the room via the window. But nothing else happened. He tried again and got another gentle gust of wind which blew the curtain. This wasn't working.

Maybe the power wasn't coming to him because he was in a confined space. Perhaps it was to prevent him from causing collateral damage. Did that mean he had to go far out of town to try out his talent, whatever it might be? Caedmon shook his head. He didn't even know how he was supposed to travel here. He hadn't prepared well for this trip, and he didn't know how to drive a car, let alone going out of town. He couldn't teleport everywhere.

His talent would be useless if he couldn't even use it. It was a waste of the Silver Blood and all the training his uncle had given him.

A spark of bright light hit the glass window and shattered it into thousands of pieces. It was like a small explosion. It was too fast for him to see what it had been, but he had a feeling it had come from him.

Then he recalled that his father's mind blades were sometimes called blades of fury because they were triggered by his anger. And because they were controlled by his mind, his father could send them wherever he wanted in whatever size he desired as long as it was in the same dimension.

It had taken his father a long time to learn how to control his mind blades. Caedmon knew he had no control whatsoever of his talent. He didn't even know exactly what it was he was capable of.

Something struck again, and the ground shook slightly. The energy was sucked out of him. The vacuum of energy sent him to the floor. He was dizzy, but he scrambled up to his feet. And then there was another round of energy loss. He dropped again. Somewhere in the back of his mind, he heard sirens.

Then he blacked out.

CHAPTER 14

Sedna hurried along the back wall of the compound where the collector stayed. She knew roughly where the security cameras were, but breaking and entering wasn't her expertise. Anatole was the expert at that. His job was to clear her way into a building. She had called Anatole and Afton, but she was here before them, and the image of Nikki's dead body enraged her. She didn't want to wait—she wanted to charge right in.

Nikki had called to tell her that the photo had been taken here, and the person in the photo was Moss. Someone didn't want Moss's involvement known. But Moss mentored Neva, and the fact that he had a clear interest in obtaining the sculpture was as clear and public to the tribe as Afton's or her own interest. This had to have been initiated by someone from outside the tribe, and Moss's connection had to involve more than just the sculpture and the leadership contest.

How could this information have leaked out so quickly? Sedna frowned and stared down at her phone. A chill ran down her spine—her phone must have been tapped. She was no technical geek, but she knew the implications of that. She realized she'd just called Afton and Anatole from this phone. She'd told them everything that happened at the clinic—and her plans.

She heard light footsteps behind her, and something brushed her shoulder. She swiveled and was about to swing a kick when she saw Anatole. Afton was right behind him.

"Stay here," Anatole said and raced along the wall to do what he always did for her—clear the path.

***

Caedmon groggily pulled himself up to his feet. He had been lying on the floor, and he wasn't sure how long he'd been out. The energy had come back into his body. He vaguely remembered feeling it trickling in bit by bit when he was in an unconscious state. Once he was up, however, it kicked in quickly.

He could think clearly now. He must have triggered his talent— some sort of a capacity for destruction. And because it was the first time, he couldn't control it and used up all of his energy in one hit. It had cost him.

Recalling the sound of sirens, he sat down on the couch and turned on the TV. The breaking news lit up the screen. A freak lightning incident had occurred on the outskirts of the city. Blurred footage from the security camera outside of a factory had captured the incident. From the sky, a rain of straight, glowing beams of light poured down with incredible force. After the first round of lightning, the ground looked like a moonscape. Gigantic holes littered the perimeter of a small forest. After the second round of lightning, the damaged ground was cut deep. The entire area was cracked and sunken. The forest looked like the Grand Canyon.

Caedmon stared with mouth open at what he had done.

He approached the broken window and looked out to the back garden. *How about gaining some control of this?* he told himself. He stared at a small decorative pond with a fountain in the middle. The water inside was frozen.

He concentrated.

A line of laser-like light beams sliced a line on the ground around the pond. Then a curtain of light surrounded it. The piece of land the pond stood on cracked apart and separated from the rest of the garden. It dropped down into the ground, vanishing into a hole the size of a large well.

Caedmon smiled.

***

Sedna and Afton followed Anatole into the grand hall of the house. In the quiet hall, she smelled the stench of fresh blood. When they entered the vault, they saw the body of the collector.

"You didn't have to kill him, Anatole!" Sedna exclaimed.

"He was in the way. Same with his guards." He pointed to a corner of the room where he had piled up five bodies.

"There's no need for a massacre here," Afton growled.

"I'm efficient. It's what you hired me for. But this," he pointed at the locked vault, "I can't help you with."

The double steel door seemed to glare at them in challenge. "Any ideas, Afton?" Sedna asked.

"Not at this stage."

They heard a cracking sound and felt the building shake slightly. "Did you feel that, or was it just me?" Anatole asked.

"Something's happening," Sedna said.

"I can help with the door," said a voice from behind. All three of them turned around, adopting fighting stances. Behind them were Moss and Neva.

"You want the sculpture for yourself, don't you?" Moss asked.

"Don't we all?" Afton stepped forward, pushing Sedna behind him.

"What did I do to upset you so much, Sedna?" Moss asked.

"You bastard." She ground her teeth and charged at him, but Afton held her back. Anatole raised his gun.

"There's no need for a fight. If you hurt Neva or me, outside of the contest, you'll be disqualified. You know that," Moss said.

"I don't care. I'll kill you!" she snarled as Afton held her back and lifted her off the ground, her legs flailing in the air.

"Calm down, Sedna. I know you're upset, but if we're hasty, nothing will be accomplished, and Nikki's death will be in vain," Afton said.

"What happened to Nikki? I talked to her just this afternoon," Neva asked, her eyes welling up with tears.

"Ask your trainer," Anatole said.

Neva turned around to look at Moss, waiting for an answer. Moss shrugged. "I have no idea what they're talking about. Now, do you want to break this door down or not?"

"I fail to see how we can collaborate. If we break in and get the sculpture, who will keep it?" Afton said.

"How about we get the sculpture to ensure the contest goes on—but no one will gain extra points," Moss suggested.

Afton nodded. "That sounds fair."

Moss nodded and approached the door. Anatole snorted. "Don't tell me you're going to rip it off with your bare hands."

Moss turned around and smirked at Anatole. "I'm going to use my brain." He pulled out a key as big as his palm from his pocket. "You'd think people would use an electronic code to lock away their valuables. But this collector is a conservative man, and he prefers the old-fashioned locks. This was in his pocket. If you'd thought to search his pockets, you would have found it."

"So why didn't you just wait until we left so you could have the sculpture for yourself?" Sedna asked.

"That was my original plan. But my righteous trainee here wanted to play fair. She said you guys got here first, and she refused to take the credit." He pointed a finger at Neva.

She shrugged.

The door was unlocked, but before they could open it, a shadow flew into the room and tackled Moss. Taken off guard, Moss fell, rolling across the floor. He regained his balance quickly as if gravity didn't work for long on him. On the floor, Keeve was scrambling to his feet.

"Keeve, no! You're not supposed to attack a trainer," Sedna called out.

Keeve's eyes were angry, and he didn't listen to her. He flew at Moss again. They fought, but Keeve was not a well-matched opponent. Keeve was soon rolling on the ground, spitting out blood.

"You give up?" Moss said. "You violated the rules, so now you're disqualified for the contest."

"I'll challenge you to the death, bastard," Keeve snarled and charged at him again.

"Do something, Afton!" Sedna said.

"There's nothing I can do, and don't you make a move, either, Sedna."

The ground grumbled, and there was a loud noise from inside the vault. Afton ran to the door and yanked it open. Inside, they saw a safe in the middle of the room. Before their eyes, a round circle cracked open on the floor around the safe. Then the floor dropped away, taking the safe with it. All that was left was a round hole in the floor.

Moss grabbed Keeve and threw him toward the hole. Keeve's head dangled over the gaping circle of darkness in the ground. Sedna and Neva flew over to grab Keeve's legs and stop him from tumbling in. They pulled him away. Then they all moved over to the hole with caution and peered down into it.

They could see straight down into the basement. The safe box had shattered, and the sculpture lay on top, glowing in the dark. Next to the statue was Caedmon. He looked up at them, "Hello there!" he said.

CHAPTER 15

Caedmon staggered along the edge of the park, his arm around Keeve to steady him as they walked. The snow was getting thicker by the minute. When they approached a bench, he let Keeve flop down onto it.

"You're heavier than you look."

"I didn't ask for your help," Keeve said.

"I didn't mean to help you. But it turned out to be the better solution for me. All I want to do is trade the sculpture for something I want in the temple."

"You'll have it tomorrow. They've moved the contest ahead because of you. Good job!"

"Look, Moss was going to kill you if I didn't make that deal. But I have no intention to keep my promise with either Moss or Afton."

"What do you mean?"

"Tell me where the temple is. I'll go there tonight to get what I want. Then I won't show up tomorrow. There will be nothing to fight for. Sedna will be fine. She won't be a leader, so then she can be with me." He grinned. Seeing Keeve's glare, he asked, "What's wrong?"

"You're an idiot."

"Hey! There's no need for insults here. Remember, I just saved you."

Keeve shook his head. "Moss killed Nikki. He deserves the worst possible death. But I'm not good enough to beat him. I never will—"

"Nikki was your girlfriend?"

Keeve shook his head again. "I wish. She was human. Mages and humans have no future together."

Caedmon's ears perked up. "Do you mean they're biologically incompatible, or that it's just a matter of tradition?"

Keeve looked up at Caedmon. "I don't really know. It just won't work."

Caedmon frowned. "All right. I'll figure that out later."

"Figure what out? Nikki's death? We can heal, but we can't bring someone back from death."

"I mean Sedna and me. But first things first, what's wrong with me going to the temple tonight?"

Keeve leaned back on the bench. "Do you think Afton and Moss let you keep the sculpture because you used that to guarantee my head and trust you to show up tomorrow?"

Caedmon shrugged. "Yes, I do."

Keeve snorted. "They aren't stupid, Caedmon. And you can't get to the temple without them—at our rank, we're not allowed to know where the temple is."

Caedmon sat down next to Keeve. "I'm an idiot."

"Don't worry. We've all been there and done that. If I'd had half a brain, I would have told Nikki I loved her."

"Why is that so important?"

"What? The love or the telling?"

"The telling bit. Wouldn't she know?"

"Have you told Sedna?" Keeve asked.

"Told her what?"

"That you love her."

"No. I haven't quantified that verb. I'm not sure I understand the magnitude of the emotion. Until I understand it, I'm not going to say it."

Keeve stared at him. "You *are* an idiot." He stood up. "And as you said, you'll figure things out." He stood and started to leave.

"So you're not going to be there tomorrow for the contest?" Caedmon asked.

"No. I withdrew, remember?"

"I mean as a spectator?" Caedmon stood up.

Keeve turned around. "You really don't get it, do you? It's not a public event. The temple is a sacred place. I'm guessing it's somewhere in the ice. You will see no one on that island tomorrow except Afton, Moss, Sedna, and Neva. And if anything happens to you there, no one on Earth would ever know."

Thinking about Eudaiz, Caedmon shrugged. "That's okay. No one needs to know where I'll be. But if I have any questions about Sedna or about mages—you know, about relationship matters—how can I find you?"

Keeve waved his hand in the air and laughed. "Oh no, I'm the last person you'd want to ask given what happened to Nikki. It will take me another hundred years to forget her and forgive myself." He turned and walked away into the darkness.

Caedmon adjusted his wrist unit and called his father. A warm beam of light brushed at his back. He turned around to see his father walking out of the teleport.

"Father, you didn't have to come. You shouldn't interact with me ..."

"I have no choice. We're having trouble with a new sub-dimension in Eudaiz. I can't free a commander I would trust to come and help you. If you want Roy or your uncle, you will have to wait for," he checked his wrist unit, "three days Earth time."

"They moved the contest up to tomorrow."

"Then mission aborted."

"No, Father. I have the sculpture. We're so close. I'll go to the contest—I don't have to fight or anything—and I'll find an opportunity to put the sculpture where it belongs. There's no other option."

"I said no. You can't handle a mission like that on your own. You're too inexperienced. Am I understood?"

Caedmon nodded. Ciaran held out two bracelets. "This is the dimensional resistance. It will lock your biological profile in at the time and space of your choice. Use one for you and one for your girl, assuming she wants to be with you. When you're done with your mission, wear them, then come and see me in Eudaiz. Understand?"

"Yes, Father."

"You'll need this." Ciaran handed Caedmon a gun. "Do *not* go to the contest tomorrow. That's an order. Nothing will go ahead without the sculpture. After I have sent the commanders and settled the plans, you can find the mages and give them an explanation for your no-show."

"I understand."

"I have to go now."

Caedmon nodded. Before stepping back into the teleport, Ciaran turned around to look at Caedmon. "As your father, I know what you're going to do. And I know I can't stop you.

Whatever happens, you have my blessing." Then the teleport disappeared.

Caedmon realized a tear had escaped his eye. He wiped it away and strode back to the hotel.

CHAPTER 16

Caedmon squeezed the scorpion sculpture in his hand. It was eerily cold. It felt as if it had a soul and was watching him, judging what he was doing. The boat trip to this isolated and icy island was long. Afton had mentioned the Earth time, but he hadn't paid much attention, so he couldn't remember. Everything around him was white and cold. He had no intention of ever coming back here, so there was no point in placing markers to trace or trying to remember anything. It was a memory he didn't want to keep.

The fate of Earth was in his hands. It was supposed to be a no-brainer. He would take the key, plug the astronomical hole, and be out of here in a heartbeat. But first, he had to lock the sculpture into the power lock for the tribe leadership contest—otherwise, the key wouldn't reveal itself. That was his plan.

He walked down the aisle of the temple as statues of whatever gods the tribe worshipped peered down on him from above. There was no religion in Eudaiz. His father said it was the best thing the council had ever established because when the citizens had no higher power to believe in, they believed in themselves and in good karma instead.

In the grand dome of the temple, Afton stood to one side, Sedna and Anatole flanking him. On the other side, Moss stood with Neva. Afton and Moss stared at each other, and it seemed more of a fight between them for the leadership than between Sedna and Neva.

Caedmon put his head down and continued walking. He couldn't care less about who won the leadership and about the internal friction of the mage tribe. It was minuscule when he considered his mission.

He glanced around quickly before approaching the altar where the sculpture would be put into the lock. It was so quiet that he swore he could hear the sound of his sweat dripping in this icy room. As he stood next to the altar, Afton said, "Caedmon, place the sculpture in the lock beneath the square plaque. You will find the base of the sculpture fits perfectly. Once it's in place, please step aside. Sedna and Neva, take your positions. Note that all the contest rules apply here. This is not a fight to the death. Do you understand?"

Sedna and Neva nodded and walked out to the middle of the room.

Caedmon approached the altar. He saw the square plaque and the lock underneath it. He held up the sculpture, pointed the base toward the hole, and plugged it in.

The temple shuddered. Snow fell from the roof and rained down in an icy dust to the courtyard outside. Caedmon stared at the sculpture. A red laser beam shone out from it. The line of light hit the wall then shot up to the ceiling and moved toward the east wing. He pulled the sculpture out of the lock. The hole glowed in alarming crimson.

"What are you doing?" Moss yelled.

A beam of dust came from the hole and hit Caedmon. He fell backward, rolling across the platform, still holding the sculpture firmly in his hand. The lock hole burned red.

"Put it back in!" Afton commanded. Anatole raised his gun, aiming at Caedmon.

Caedmon thrust the sculpture in front of him. "Approach me, and I'll destroy your precious sculpture," he said and pulled out his gun, pointing it at the sculpture.

"You tricked us. You always wanted the sculpture!" Neva cried.

"No, Neva. I don't want your sculpture. But it must serve a higher purpose than being plugged into that lock. I'm sorry, but neither of you is going to have any leadership today."

He withdrew toward the hallway leading to the east wing. The group approached him slowly.

"You're not going to destroy the sculpture, are you?" Afton asked.

"No, I need it to get my key."

"Your family key is in this temple?" Sedna asked.

"Yes, I wasn't lying about that. I need the sculpture to see it. It's very important."

Sedna let out a sigh of relief, and that hurt him because he was still lying to her. She had no idea what was ahead.

Sedna said to Afton, "Why don't we let him take his key? Then we'll put the sculpture back where it's supposed to be."

"It doesn't look as if we have any other option," Afton said.

"Do you swear not to destroy it?" Moss asked.

"I swear," Caedmon said. "I need the key. If you let me get it, then no one will get hurt."

"If that's all you want, why didn't you tell us before? We could have negotiated. It didn't have to come to this," Afton told him.

"Do you honestly think your people would have been open to a discussion about me using your sculpture? You fought for it for centuries. Do you think you could have gotten your people to agree to lend it to me?"

"He's right, Afton. Let him do what he needs to do. My gun will guarantee he doesn't take the sculpture out of this temple," Anatole said.

Caedmon looked at the group. When it appeared they had no further objection, he turned around and dashed down the corridor to the east wing, following the red line on the ceiling. Everyone raced after him, but they kept their distance.

CHAPTER 17

The east wing was grand and mysterious. The red light beamed across the ceiling and down to the far wall. In the middle of the wall, a secret compartment the size of a large cabinet had opened. Inside the compartment stood a life-sized statue of a scorpion. In the middle of the scorpion head, there was a large eye with a transparent eyelid. Via the eyelid, Caedmon could see the Scorpio key glowing in crimson.

He turned toward the group approaching him. "Stay right there."

They stopped in their tracks.

Caedmon concentrated. He could do this. This was his first mission. It might be his last, but he had to do this. He looked at Sedna. Catching his look and reading his mind, she approached, but Afton pulled her back.

Caedmon closed his eyes, switched his Silver Blood on, and wielded his mind light beams. They came. Thousands of them. Like stars in the sky. They formed into hard beams of incredible force outside the temple. In his mind's eye, he drew a circle in the snow around the temple. He grunted as this directive sucked much of the energy out of him. Thousands of light beams dug into the snow.

Blood trickled from his nose. His knees buckled as the temple shook with the force outside. He braced himself against the wall. "This temple is going to sink. Leave," he said. Then he punched the eyelid of the scorpion statue. It opened, and he pulled the Scorpio key out, placing the sculpture inside. The eyelid slammed shut and sealed instantly.

Afton and Moss charged at the statue. Caedmon pointed the gun at them.

"Leave. Now!" he told Neva, Sedna, and Anatole.

The temple shook as if in an earthquake. They heard the first crack in the icy ground outside. All of the glass doors and windows shattered from the force.

"Leave, Sedna! Right now!" Caedmon shouted at her.

"No."

"Let's go. We can talk outside," Neva said. She was already halfway to the door. Anatole pulled at Sedna's arm, but she broke free of his grip.

Moss and Afton rushed toward Caedmon. Afton fought Caedmon, and Moss ran to the scorpion statue, trying to open the eyelid. Afton left Caedmon and tackled Moss. Afton and Moss fought each other like mad dogs.

Neva had gone through the door. The ceilings cracked as the foundation of the temple shook. Anatole let go of Sedna and followed Neva outside.

Caedmon ran toward the statue to make sure Afton and Moss had not broken the eyelid. They were still fighting. And by Caedmon's gauge, this fight would take a while. Only if he buried this temple beneath the seabed would the statue be safe as well as the sculpture inside it.

Sedna ran toward him.

"No, no, Sedna. Go away!" Caedmon shouted at her.

"I won't go without you." She pulled at him.

Caedmon knew he didn't have much energy left in him. He knew what he had done. He had used up his Silver Blood energy in one round. He had to switch back to human form, rest, then use another round of Silver Blood to heal his body. It wouldn't be so problematic for other Silver Blood users, but due to his lack of experience, it was the only thing he could think of. But switching back to human form right now was a very bad idea.

The temple sank a bit more, and water began to seep in. Moss and Afton continued to fight. Caedmon snatched Sedna and flung her over his shoulders. As weak as he was, with his Silver Blood on, he was still much too strong for her to resist.

He darted to the doorway and ran through it. As soon as they hit the edge of the crack in the ice, he tossed her over to the other side. He stepped back inside at the exact time the temple dipped, sank, and became totally submerged in the icy water.

CHAPTER 17

Sedna screamed. In front of her was a large pool of the Arctic Sea. The temple had disappeared from sight. And so had Afton and Caedmon. "Caedmon!" she cried out, although she knew it was hopeless. "Caedmon!" she called again.

She dipped her hand into the water. She would freeze to death before she could get to anyone down there. No human could survive the icy water. But Afton and Caedmon weren't human. She strained her eyes, hoping to see them break through the surface of the calm water.

There was nothing.

She thought of Caedmon, and her heart ached. She hadn't had a chance to tell him she had forgiven him for leaving her. She had no family. No friends. And now, no mentor. She didn't care what kind of creature Caedmon was. She wanted him to know that the time she'd spent with him four years ago were the best memories she had ever had in her life.

***

Under the water, Caedmon held his breath and swam deep inside the temple. He had to make sure Moss and Afton hadn't cracked the eyelid and taken out the sculpture. He had nothing left of the Silver Blood in this round. He'd had no choice but to switch it off. He swam in the deep water of the Arctic Sea as a human.

He headed into the east wing and saw the last round of the fight between Moss and Afton. They were incredible creatures. Energy sparked in the deep blue water. Caedmon would take Afton's side if he could. But it wasn't for him to decide.

Moss's hand savaged the jugular in Afton's neck in his last attack. Afton's body floated in the water, flowing past Caedmon with his eyes still open. Dead eyes. *I'm sorry,* Caedmon thought. He clung to a large rock, keeping out of sight so Moss didn't see him. He knew he had no chance fighting him.

But Moss was a mage, not a fish. Caedmon knew he would have to be quick to get the sculpture and then get up to the surface. Moss turned toward the scorpion eyelid and punched hard. Energy sparked. Caedmon wasn't sure how long it would hold.

He swam around until he found a loose piece of ice on a broken wall above Moss. He pushed at it. It moved about an inch. He pushed more. And more. Moss paid no attention to him. He was intent on cracking the eyelid. Caedmon used the last drop of his human breath and pushed again. It wasn't enough.

He tried to turn his eudqi back on, but he was so weak, it didn't work. He turned back toward the ice. He thought of his parents. He recalled the devastated look in his father's eyes when he told him he'd decided to take on this mission. He didn't even want to think about how his mother would react.

And now this. Mission unaccomplished.

He closed his eyes. He was a human with a family to think about. He was a son, not a Silver Blood soldier. And he might have been a good lover, once. He couldn't let it end here, like this. He pushed one last time.

The ice piece fell down, crushed Moss and covered the scorpion.

Running out of breath, Caedmon looked up. He saw the dim light of the surface and knew it was a long way to the light. He pushed up with his feet. His body was numb. He couldn't feel much. But he kept kicking. And pushing. Above the water, in the dim light, he saw the silhouette of Sedna, bending over the water, waiting for him.

It was so close and yet so far to the surface. To her.

He kicked again, but his body didn't move any further. He could feel nothing. He knew he was drowning.

CHAPTER 19

Sedna couldn't believe her eyes. Beneath the surface the dark blue sea, she saw a shadow. It was Caedmon. He was trying to resurface. She bent down right at the edge of the ice, waiting to catch him. But then he slowed down.

"Come on, Caedmon. Come on."

He slowed even more. And about five feet below the surface, he stopped.

She dipped her body down into the water like a seal, snatched his collar before he sank, and yanked him up onto the ice.

He barely breathed. His lips had turned purple. And she was willing to bet his internal organs has started to turn into ice.

She gathered her light. "Come on, Caedmon, stay with me." His body had rejected her light before. But hell, she had to try. She held his hands and pushed the energy in. This time, his body soaked it up like sunshine. She felt so deliriously happy she almost giggled out loud. She wrapped him up in her arms and let her warm energy pour into him.

After a while, she felt the natural warmth of his body returning. She heard his strong heartbeat and even breathing.

Then something happened—his own supernatural defense mechanism kicked in. And as she had anticipated, it zapped her. She dropped him to the snow and laughed. She was pleased that she had been right the whole time. He wasn't human. She just hadn't realized his supernatural power could be switched on and off like this.

But she was pleased he was alive. He opened his eyes.

"Hey," she said and brushed a stray wisp of hair from his forehead. She smiled.

He smiled back.

She glanced back at the water and then looked back at Caedmon. Now that she knew Caedmon was alive, she thought of Afton. Regardless of how strict he was with her training, regardless of his motive in taking her under his wing, he had been like her father. All he ever wanted was to be the mentor of the leader. She saw nothing wrong with that.

A tear rolled down her face. "How did he die?"

Caedmon struggled but managed to sit up. "I'm sorry. Moss had already killed him when I went back down."

"How do I know you didn't kill them both?"

Caedmon got to his feet. He swayed, and she had to hold him. "You don't have to believe me, Sedna. I lied to you, so I don't expect you to trust me ever again. But I didn't kill Afton. Moss did. I killed Moss."

She wiped the tears from her face. "It doesn't matter now. He's dead."

"It does matter. I need you to understand why I'm doing what I'm doing." He held her shoulders. "It's for a greater cause, and if it means I have to live with your wrath, so be it. The key isn't an antique item, and I am not a treasure hunter. The key holds the power, and if it gets into the wrong hands, the multiverse— I mean, people will die."

"And you're saying you're the rightful owner of the key?"

Caedmon shook his head. "It's not for me. It will be kept in a safe place. The position of the scorpion statue had to be kept a secret. If someone pulled the sculpture out..." He paused. "Forget it... You're smart, and I know you can take the truth. The sculpture was needed to plug an astronomical hole. If the hole were exposed, it would destroy Earth. It's as simple as that. Everyone living on this little planet would die."

She frowned. "You consider Earth little?"

He nodded. "It is compared to where I come from. And before you ask, yes, I'm technically human. I just don't live here."

"So you're alien?"

He smiled. "I don't like that term, but if you need to label me, I guess it fits. As for my special power, I can control it, like switching it on and off. But when it's on, I have a weak point. If that point is hit, it could be fatal."

"And that's where I kicked you in the hotel?"

He nodded. "Not exactly, but it was close."

"If that's your fatal point, why are you telling me?"

He pointed to the right side of his chest. "I have my power on now to heal my injuries. It's right here. You can kill me by hitting me right here, right now."

She touched his chest, where she had kicked him before, and felt a lump in her throat. "Do you trust me that much?"

He nodded. "Not only do I trust you, but I want you to come with me to where I live. You have no family here. And because of this mission, I'll be separated from my family. We can be together, Sedna. We'll be happy. I want to be with you."

She smiled.

They heard a noise and then footsteps. Anatole stepped out from behind a rock with a gun in his hand which he pointed at them. "Not so fast. Go wherever you like, but the key stays with me. I know you have a super power, Caedmon. But as you've said, you're recuperating. You're weak. And I don't think any power that exists can save you from a bullet in the head."

"Are you working for Hoyt Flanagan? What did he promise you?" Caedmon asked.

"A lot. Nothing you could ever match. Now put the key down and step back. I would have shot you already, but Sedna was in the way."

Sedna stepped in front of Caedmon. "In your way? Like this?"

Caedmon pushed Sedna aside. "Don't do this, Sedna," he said.

Anatole clucked his tongue. "I'm only interested in the key. Put it down, and I won't shoot either of you. But don't try my patience."

"If you take the key to the wrong person, a lot of people will die, Anatole," Sedna said.

He laughed. "I kill people for a living, Sedna."

"And the sculpture? Your client wants that, too?" Caedmon asked.

"Yes, but I'll worry about that later. Now, put the key down."

"If you take the sculpture, it will destroy Earth. And that will kill you, too," Caedmon said.

"Yeah, I heard that part. But I'm not going to live here, so it's not my concern. If you say one more word without putting that key down, I'll blow your head off, Caedmon."

CHAPTER 20

Blood rained down on Caedmon and Sedna as Anatole's head exploded.

From behind a rock, Neva stepped out, holstered her gun, and grinned. "Before you jump, keep your key. I don't want it."

"What about the sculpture?" Sedna narrowed her eyes.

Neva laughed. "You were certainly out of touch with the tribe business. The sculpture is a symbol of leadership only if there is competition."

"You never beat me in a contest, Neva."

"True. I never beat you when it comes to scuffling."

"Martial arts."

"Whatever." Neva patted her gun. "But when it comes to using guns, you're likely to shoot your own foot."

"Are you that bad?" Caedmon raised an eyebrow at Sedna.

"I don't like guns," she snapped. Then she turned to Neva. "You want me to give up the leadership without a fight?"

Neva shrugged. "I hate martial arts. I could have taken you out with my gun. But I didn't. So let me make it easy for you. You don't want the leadership. You just want your guy."

Caedmon smiled.

"Excuse me!" Sedna exclaimed.

"Come on. It's been four years. You've turned down dates. You kept the same stupid handkerchief and beat the crap out of a pickpocket when he tried to snatch it. I always thought you were being ridiculous, but now that I see him, I think he's worth it. So go with him—and leave the tribe to me." Neva grinned again as Sedna's jaw dropped.

"You spied on me?" Sedna raised her voice.

Caedmon bit back a laugh and said nothing.

"Do we have a deal? Or do you want a real fight?"

Caedmon touched Sedna's shoulder. "Come on, leave with me."

"You see the price I have to pay for this?" Sedna said, pointing at Neva.

"I'll compensate you. Come on. Let's go," Caedmon said.

"What kind of compensation?"

"Whatever you want."

"I'll hold you to that." Sedna circled her finger around a spot on Caedmon's chest. Neva shrugged and walked away.

***

The double steel door slid open, revealing a round station at the grand control center of

Eudaiz. Caedmon held Sedna's hand and walked in. His heart skipped a beat when he saw his father turn to him from a monitor at which he was working. He would have felt more comfortable meeting at home rather than here. The scene in front of them was a bit intimidating. But to his surprise, Sedna's hand was steady. She was as calm as the still Arctic water had been.

"Sedna Aardel, it's a pleasure to meet you," Ciaran said and bent down to give her a hug. He winced, absently putting a hand on his left side as he stood back up.

"The pleasure is mine. Caedmon has explained the situation, and I understand."

Ciaran nodded. "I'm glad."

"You're injured. Do you want me to heal you?" Sedna asked.

"What? When?" Caedmon asked.

"Thank you. My injury is minor, and it will heal by the time I get to my bed tonight. My wife won't even know what happened during the day." Ciaran smiled.

"Please don't tell me you got injured because of this mission. I told you I could handle it myself," Caedmon said.

"When you broke protocol and went ahead with the fight at the temple, I had to interfere, not as your king but as your father," Ciaran growled.

"You couldn't round up your commanders in time. We had no intelligence in Xiilok to do anything remotely. So whatever you did, it had to be direct. Please don't tell me you went there by yourself." Caedmon stared at Ciaran. "You did! Oh dear the multiversal god! What if something had happened to you? What am I going to tell Mother?" Caedmon raked his fingers through his hair and paced the room.

"Nothing is worse than what you would do to her if you failed this mission," Ciaran said.

"What did you do in Xiilok?" Sedna asked.

"I broke into their control center, hacked the system, and replaced the contracts Hoyt has made with people on Earth regarding the Scorpio key. I basically told the contractors the deal is off, on Hoyt's behalf, of course. I only had time to handle three contracts. By the time they figure out the signals were fake, it'll be over. The key will be where it should be." Ciaran reached his hand out, palm up.

Caedmon placed the key into his father's hand. Ciaran turned and locked the key in the vault with codes that might take Caedmon a million years to figure out.

"What are the contracts you canceled?" Sedna asked.

"Moss, Anatole, and Neva," Ciaran said as he was working on his monitor.

"Neva!" Sedna exclaimed.

Ciaran stopped typing and returned. "Yes. What's the problem?"

"So she knew the deal was off, she shot Anatole to gain Sedna's trust, and she bluffed Sedna to give up the leadership without a fight," Caedmon said.

"Wicked. I'm sorry, Sedna," Ciaran said.

"No worries—the leadership doesn't mean much to me anymore," she said.

Ciaran smiled and glanced at the bracelets that both Caedmon and Sedna were wearing. "I can see you both chose to lock in your profiles. You'll remain at this age and make for a very long time. This time resistance should be fine for a brief visit. You should go back to your future time."

"That's too soon, Father. Would you like me to help finding the other keys?" Caedmon asked. Seeing the look on his father's face, he muttered, "Guess that's a no."

Sedna smiled. "I think it's time to go." She kissed Ciaran goodbye and turned on her heel.

"She's a keeper," Ciaran said.

Caedmon smiled. "Thank you, Father." He shook his father's hand, then before his father could react, he pulled his father in for a hug.

Then he turned around, followed Sedna back to his future.

CHAPTER 21

It had been a year since they had been married, and today he had received the best news ever: he was going to be a father.

In front of a control panel inside his private chamber, he glanced at the report of the seven stations he was handling as part of the practice his father had assigned him in preparation for his commander role.

He chuckled to himself. His father had been conceived during the Red Stage of the Daimon Gate and had lived his whole life under the pressure of being the best creature in the multiverse. Caedmon had also been conceived during the Red Stage. It was worse for him, however, because on top of his biological and ontological make, he had his father to live up to.

No matter how much his father tried to lessen the pressure, Caedmon always felt it whenever anyone in the multiverse laid eyes on him. And in those unfortunate encounters, he had promised himself a thousand times over that he would never make his children go through what he had been through.

Now it was time to prove he could keep his promises.

Father! Imagining the word rolling off the tongue of his child, he smiled.

He closed the report on the screen and switched to a plantation station nearby. He wasn't in charge of that station, but he had a friend living there, and he had been working on a very special kind of flower for Sedna. The flowers hadn't blossomed yet, but he would harvest them now as a present for her. He sent his friend a message and was about to leave when he saw a red flag at a gateway on the screen.

"No!" He opened the gateway's log and disliked what he saw before he could even see it clearly. Sedna had broken the seal, passed the time traveling gate, which she didn't have permission to do, and traveled to the past.

He called her communicator. "What are you doing, Sedna? Where are you going?" The signal bounced. He shook his head. She had passed the gate and had obviously turned off her communication unit. She didn't want to be tracked.

"Come on, come on!"

His fingers flew over the keyboard, accessing more data, and there it was. On the screen was her last message to his father.

"Request access to Ciaran LeBlanc. Matter: private. Priority: code red - urgent. Content: Meet me at Ice Station with the Scorpio key. Now. Your time."

He stormed out of the control room and charged toward the time traveling chamber. The technology was new and needed improvement, but he'd have to take his chances. He triangulated the time stamp of the message, the time in Eudaiz, and the current time in Iilos and figured out the time and place to which Sedna had traveled. Math had never been his friend, but he hoped his calculations were accurate. He had no choice but to trust they were.

He made a prediction and entered commands into the machine. It shuddered, and the engine came to life. In no time, he walked out into the middle of the Ice Station.

The chill breeze blasted at his face. This was part of the transitional zone of the multiverse. It belonged to no one. No authority. No governance. And of course, no justice system.

In the distance, he saw a couple of shadows on the icy white surface. On Earth, the white stuff would have been snow. He wasn't sure what it was here, but Sedna had chosen this location for a reason.

"Sedna!" he called out.

Sedna and Ciaran looked at him. Then, when his father was turned toward him, Sedna hit him in the head with what looked like the Scorpio key. As Ciaran toppled to the ground, Sedna turned around and ran away.

He had many talents. But flying wasn't one of them. Caedmon ran as fast as he could over the icy ground. In the meantime, Ciaran had groggily risen to his feet and was chasing after Sedna.

Sedna had grown up in the snow. She had told him many stories about her homeland. As much as he loved her, those stories were too much like fairy tales to him. He hadn't accepted them as hard facts.

Snow and ice. *What had she said about them?*

He kept running, but he couldn't close the distance enough to have a conversation with his father. Ciaran kept running after Sedna, and she kept darting away, remaining just out of reach.

Caedmon came to a skidding halt as he remembered the twisted version of Snow White Sedna had told him. Snow White knew the apple was poisoned, but she took it so that the evil queen couldn't hurt anyone else.

Sedna was running away with the Scorpio key. He could think of only one reason right now why she was doing this, and he had to act on it. He used his strongest talent and willed a mind blade. With the blade, he cut into the piece of ice in front of his father to stop him from following Sedna.

Ciaran turned and looked at him. Sedna stopped running, looked at him one last time, and then jumped into a dimensional gateway of an ice oblivion hole. A massive explosion erupted from the hole, blowing Ciaran backward and sending him sliding across the ice.

Caedmon scrambled toward his father. Ciaran wasn't conscious. He tossed him over his shoulders and charged toward a flying capsule. Shortly, they arrived at Tower Three, an exclusive area of the king Sciphil healing chamber. The computer shouted for the access code, and he placed his father's palmprint on the control panel to gain access.

Once inside, he placed his father into the chamber. A computer voice intoned, "You are injured, Sciphil Three. The healing process will commence immediately."

The round glass door shut, and the healing chamber spun like a small tornado.

Ciaran stirred and regained consciousness then ordered the chamber to stop and signaled Caedmon to come in.

"Father, the healing process hasn't finished. It's taxing to stop it midway."

"Caedmon, come here."

"No, I have to reactivate this. Will it take my command?"

"Caedmon."

"Yes, Father?"

"Come here."

He did as his father asked and sat down next to the raised bench where Ciaran lay.

"I'm sorry about Sedna," Ciaran said.

The emotion hit Caedmon like a storm. He buried his head in his hands and let it all out. He felt Ciaran's hand on his head, but it gave him no comfort. He would never be able to control his emotions like his father. He knew crying was weak. But he couldn't stop himself.

After a while, he looked up and found Ciaran looking at him, waiting. "It's unlikely Sedna would survive the blast," his father said. "I'm sorry, Caedmon. She said the key was fake and that she wanted you to find the real one. I didn't expect the blast, and I don't understand why she said it was her fault."

"She's a mage. She knows many things we don't. If I go back to Earth and fix this, do you think it will change anything?"

"You have already manipulated the past to get the key, and that's what caused the unfortunate incident just now. I don't think you can do it twice. But if Sedna wants us to find the real key, then we will."

"She didn't say we, did she? She wanted me to do it. So I'll find the real key. I'll find the reason behind all this. And I will kill whoever caused this."

"I should tell you revenge doesn't change anything, but I would be lying. Because it does give you resolution and closure. I'll need you back here to take your commander position and manage the district where you are much needed."

"Then I'll go now." At the door, he turned and asked, "Do you believe Snow White knew the apple was poisoned but still took it so that the evil queen couldn't hurt anyone else?"

Ciaran shook his head. "I'd kill the queen before she even had a chance to come close to Snow White."

Caedmon nodded and left Tower Three to go back to his time traveling chamber. People always said time healed everything, but because he had time traveled for the greater good, he'd gotten his wife killed.

He didn't need time to help him heal. He would use time to kill whoever had caused him pain and robbed him of his family.

The End

About the Author

D.N. Leo is an Australian author. She writes urban fantasy and supernatural thrillers, and has published several series in the Multiverse Collection. She is an award winning author, an accomplished film director and a passionate advocate of social cause and human rights. She lives in Melbourne with her beloved husband, a polite dog and a sarcastic cat.

For a short period of time, D.N. Leo gives away several books and audiobooks in the Multiverse Collection.

Find out more on her website

http://dnleo.com

Light of Demon and

Ash of Scorpio

© copyright 2017 D.N. Leo

BLOODSTONE TRILOGY

by D.N Leo

Website: http://dnleo.com

Prequel: ASH OF SCORPIO

Book 1: LIGHT OF DEMON

Book 2: SHADOW OF ANGEL

Book 3: SHADE OF DARKNESS

For a limited time, D.N. Leo gives away
Several e-books and audiobooks in the Multiverse
Collection

VISIT THE WEBSITE AND CLAIM YOUR BOOKS
http://dnleo.com

THANK YOU FOR READING!
D.N. LEO

D.N. LEO 'S NOVELS
SERIES READING ORDER

http://dnleo.com

A SHADE OF MIND
The Journey from Earth to Eudaiz
Main Characters: Ciaran, Madeline, Tadgh, and Jo
(Recommended reading in order)
1-4 Random Psychic
2-4 Forever Mortal
3-4 Elusive Beings
4-4 Imperfect Divine

—

MINDSCAPE
Main characters:
Ciaran, Madeline, Tadgh, Jo, Kyle, Hoyt, Ayana, Pete,
Sizx, Lorcan, Orla
(Recommended reading in order within series, can be
read in ANY order in related to other series)

Queen's Gambit
Knight & Pawn
Lone Castle
Doubled Bishops
Dead Squares
King's Endgame

—

SPECTRUM OF LIES
Main characters: Lorcan, Orla, Roy and Mori
(Recommended reading in order)
1-4 White Curse - Negotiate Death
2-4 Blue Fox - Befriend a Rogue
3-4 Indigo Stone - Cheat a Sorcerer
4-4 Red Moon - Break a Curse
—

SILVER BLOOD
Main characters:
Ciaran, Madeline, Tadgh, Jo, Caedmon, Sedna, Roy,
Mori, Zach, Mya, Lorcan and Orla
This series can be read in ANY order within the series
and in related to other series.

Virgo
Libra
Scorpio

THE GOOD DEITY
Main characters:
Main characters: Mya Portman, Zach Flynn, Leon,
Kirra.
This series can be read in ANY order within the series
and in related to other series.
Almost Countable
Almost Sure
Almost Everywhere

DARK SOLAR

Main characters:

Main characters: Dinah, Arik, Ciaran and Madeline

Oleander

Wolfsbane

Maikoa